Feeling His Passion

MW00944151

Empathic Shifters Book 1

By

CJ Jones

Copyright © 2018 CJ Jones

All rights reserved.

ISBN: 1981194215
ISBN: 978-1981194216

HAPPY
READING

DEDICATION

I dedicate this book to my wonderful supporative husband David (Bear). Without who's support this book would have not been finished. To my mentor Kate Douglas who was there to answer all of my crazy late-night questions and who talked me back from the ledge, several times in the past 10 years. This book was a labor of love 10 years in the making. To my many beta readers who helped me be consistent.

Editor/Proofreader: Kim Huther

www.wordsmithproofreading.wordpress.com

Cover Design: Dar Albert

www.wickedsmartdesigns.com

Blurb: Anette King

www.theblurbdiva.com

Chapter 1

Mt. Charleston, Las Vegas, NV

The sun appeared over Sunrise Mountain, casting an orange glow low in the morning sky. Across the valley on Mt. Charleston, Jake Carrington sat high in a tree. Silently, he waited for his prey to approach along the path below. The air on Mt. Charleston was crisp, perfect for deer hunting.

Jake pulled his senses close to the surface. He heard the occasional chirps of birds. He inhaled the fragrances of fresh rosemary, sage, and pine. There it was, a scent. It preceded the incoming prey. The sound of hooves far off in the distance gradually moved closer toward his location. He felt the vibrations flow from the ground, up through tree, into his body.

Jake remembered the weekends his grandfather would take him hunting during deer season. He always felt more alive then. Time spent out of the city always recharged his batteries. Pop-Pop taught him to pay close attention to nature.

He invited three of his Marine buddies to hunt with him: RL, Robert from Colorado, and Alex from Connecticut. They were more than just friends—they were his brothers.

Jake and RL were childhood friends. They met Alex and Robert in boot camp. Jake and RL always felt when something had happened to each other, good or bad. The moment they shook hands, Jake and RL knew who and what they were. Empathic Shifters.

Empathic Shifters were born with a spirit animal that could sense and feel each other's emotions, whether they were family or close friends. They also could shift into their spirit animals when called upon. As fate would have it, their spirit animals were wolves. A connection that made them more than just fast friends, and closer than family.

Jake felt restless. Lately, he felt that there had to be more to life than this, hanging with the boys and hunting every season. Slowly, over the last five years, loneliness began to set in. He felt maybe it wasn't *something* he was missing, but more *someone*.

A small bite of cold wind blew across Jake's skin, which brought him back to the present. The wind said something to him in a familiar voice. It sounded like his grandfather. His Pop-Pop always said: "Pup, if you hear the wind, listen to it. Nature might be trying to tell you something important." The voice today sounded louder than usual, and this time it sounded like a man's voice, just like his grandfather's voice had been.

Jake shook off the feeling and refocused on the hunt. His Uncle Jonathan and his grandfather taught him patience when hunting. He learned to sit still and wait for the prey to come to him. He learned to control his breathing, steady his heartbeat, and to stay alert at all times. Mother Nature could change at any moment and send the prey off into another direction.

He saw his breath in the cold air. Every part of his body remained still, except his eyes. RL also sat in a tree, thirty yards away to his right. Across from him and to the right of RL was Alex, another thirty yards away. Robert sat to Jake's left. The perfect viewpoint. Each could see anything that came in from any direction. The ideal kill zone.

Deer frequently came to this spot to graze. It was the perfect location for them. As the vibrations became stronger, he didn't have to look at his friends. They felt the same, as his body remained perfectly still. Jake moved just his eyes down and to the right where he spotted his prey. It walked between RL and himself. A beautiful six-point buck, bigger than the normal ones in the region. Jake only moved his eyes as the animal came into view.

They all held their weapons at the ready, but Jake seemed to have a better angle. Jake barely breathed, his heartrate almost at a standstill. Slow and steady, the prey entered the clearing, fifteen feet below them. Jake positioned his bow with a slow and steady aim. The prey stopped to clear snow from the ground to reveal the grass underneath. Jake's eyes were steady on his prey. Slowly, he took aim. Inhaled deep, exhaled slow, and loosed his arrow. No sound was made as the arrow flew true and hit its target directly in the heart. The large buck dropped to the ground without a sound.

Chapter 2

“Cocktails, coffee,” Cathryn said as she served her customers in her assigned slot area at the Preserve Resort and Casino. Cathryn Harvey and her best friend of twenty years, Patty, began working at the casino shortly after they served eight years together in the U.S. Navy.

Working there had its interesting moments. It was exciting at first, but that wore off quickly. Gamblers tend to be a little too touchy-feely, rude, or plain obnoxious.

She wanted more from life than slinging drinks. With a Bachelor’s degree in Information Technology, the sky was the limit with her new career. Although which sky, she had no clue yet.

Cathryn released a slow exhale as she set her tray on the bar.

“Rough out there tonight?” Patty nodded toward the patrons.

Cathryn exhaled. “Yes, it is. Tips are great, but if that shit-faced guy sitting in High-Limit slots doesn’t stop trying to grab my uniform tail? Security will be the least of his problems.”

Patty leaned close to Cathryn and whispered, “Now, Cat, you can’t shift and eat the customers, even if they deserve it. The beverage manager frowns on such things, and you know how much security hates filling out all the paperwork that comes with such matters. Not good.”

With an exaggerated sigh of aggravation, Cat replied, “Yeah, I know. But we both know I’d be doing the world a favor by killing off that asshole and ending his bloodline.”

She inhaled deeply and exhaled slowly, “I’m out of here in four hours and finally on my way home with two days off.”

"Lucky you, I still have five more hours to go."

Shirley, another waitress, petite with curly blond hair that cascaded down her back, walked up to the station and overheard their conversation.

"I don't know how you two do it every day. Thirty miles each way is too far for me to drive for work."

"True, but it's so worth it. When we get home to our big, old, beautiful log cabin secluded in the mountains, we have absolute peace and quiet," Cathryn said.

"You're all alone up there, without company," Shirley replied.

"We have company. Four Alaskan Malamutes," Cathryn responded.

"Our wolf substitutes. Since the boss won't let us take a wolf pair home. I mean, really, we have more than enough property for them to roam. But you know the city's regulations. I tell you, the human race has no sense of humor…"

Cathryn nudged Shirley.

"Besides, you know my feelings on men lately. They're all pigs and deserve to die."

Patty gave Cathryn a look that said, 'shame on you'.

Cathryn rolled her eyes then continued.

"Okay, not all of them are pigs that deserve to die. Some of them are dogs that deserve to be slaves. But the pigs, the pigs deserve to die!"

Cathryn looked up, and in a low voice, said, "Speaking of one who deserves to become a slave, here comes Roger."

Roger, the bar manager, a short, middle-aged, pale-faced balding man with a Napoleonic attitude, approached the bar. "Ladies," he began with his usual condescending tone.

"Roger," Cathryn and Patty replied in perfect sarcastic unison. Their sarcastic response did not go unnoticed by him because he responded with a slightly dirty look.

"Cathryn, I'm going to need you to pick up the lounge. And only cover half of your slot area. Patty, I need you to cover the rest of Cathryn's slot area, which includes High-Limit slots. Sandy went home sick again today."

"Am I still out of here at ten?" Cathryn asked

"Yes; I can't authorize any overtime tonight, ladies."

***

Jake and the guys carried the kill back to his cabin. They had it dressed and quartered within two hours. Jake claimed the liver as his prize for the kill. RL claimed the heart, while Robert and Alex shared the hide. They split the meat between them. Since Alex and Robert lived out of state, Jake promised to ship their share.

He made dinner reservations at the preserve's steakhouse. As part owner, he didn't need reservations, but letting them know in advance allowed the staff to set up the private room if he wanted it. His uncle made him a full partner and owner of the casino after he left the Marines seven years ago. They showered, dressed casually, and were on the road by 5 pm.

As Jake and the boys walked through the casino, every woman's head turned in their direction and sniffed the air. The pheromone levels of a male shifter increased during a hunt. The rich cologne-like aroma trailed from the parking garage through the casino, into the steakhouse. Every woman in the place was affected. Even those who had male companions couldn't help but stare. Jake decided not to use the private room but sat at a big table in the middle of the steakhouse. They enjoyed and pretended to ignore the attention, as well as the glances from all the admiring women.

After dinner, they walked to the lounge located outside the steakhouse and found a table.

"Jake, that was smooth the way you nailed that buck. Seriously, a thing of beauty, brother," Alex said.

"Yeah, man, right in the heart. You completely missed the shoulder blade," added Robert.

"I had forgotten how great you were with a bow," said RL.

He and the guys talked about hunting with rifles. He'd always been a great shot with a gun or handgun, but his real forte had always been with the bow and arrow. He felt that hunting should be done the old-fashioned way.

They talked, laughed, joked, when a breeze crossed his nose that carried a scent. He'd crossed its path before in the casino but only small whiffs here and there. This time the scent was stronger, soft and feminine. It stirred strong feelings in his being. His body became alive, a tingling sensation spread around him like a blanket. This time he inhaled deeply as the sensation in and round his body increased. The scent was like a burst of jasmine, lilac, and lavender. He looked around to see who that sweet smell belonged to.

He turned toward the lounge bar and saw her standing at the cocktail station. He saw a better view of her when she turned toward him. She was tall, toned, and the most beautiful woman he'd ever seen. Questions formed in his mind.

'Where the hell had she been all his life? How long had she been working here?'

His senses sharpened as he took in her features. Her skin looked smooth, like silky dark caramel. He licked his lips, anticipating how she might taste. Curly black hair shone like the night sky. Deep amber eyes. She walked from around the bar and up the small stairs toward him. Jake liked the way she walked. No, not walked. Strutted. She had a strut. She carried herself like a queen who ruled all she surveyed.

He was able to see the rest of her, full round breasts, small waist with hips that begged to be held from behind. Her lips were full, juicy, shiny, and designed for kissing. She wore her uniform as if it were tailor-made for her perfect body.

Jake made eye contact with her as she walked past him. She smiled then proceeded to the tables to the back of the lounge. He had the perfect view of her ass. "Now, that is an ass to nibble on," he muttered under his breath. Her uniform tail did something to him. His wolf stood up and took notice, as did other parts of his anatomy. His wolf wanted to play with her, now! Her scent called to them loud and clear. His wolf said MINE!!! And Jake agreed.

RL snapped his fingers in front of Jake's ear.

"Hey, brother, you might want to leave her some clothes on. She could catch her death from cold."

Jake whipped his head around. "Huh? What?"

"You didn't hear a single word we said, did you?" Alex accused.

"No, he didn't. Bro, we were saying thank you for inviting us this weekend to go hunting and hang out like we used to when we were in the Corps," Robert said.

Jake momentarily turned his attention from the woman.

"It's no problem. I missed you guys. You know *mi casa es su casa*. Anytime you need a place to stay or just hang out. You have it."

He turned just as she walked to their table and fixated on her eyes. They were like jeweled amber set in precious settings, just cleaned, polished, and just beautiful.

***

Cathryn stood at the cocktail station, cleared her tray of empty glasses and beer bottles when a scent wafted across her nose. She had smelled that same scent before. Every now and then, depending on what area she worked, that scent would send a tingling sensation throughout her body. It was a scent of musk, like the forest after a good summer rain, it was enticing.

Back then it was just faint, it was there then gone. At the time, Cathryn chalked it up to the fact she had not been with a man since she and He Who Shall Not Be Named broke up. But today it was strong and completely grabbed her attention and would not let go.

"Are you okay?" Patty asked

Cathryn came out of her trance.

"Yes, no. That was weird. It was like my body went on alert. Remember that rush, the hairs standing up on your skin during drills at sea? But this is a different kind of rush."

Cathryn felt more arousal than adrenaline. Her heart rate and body temperature increased, she felt moist in her lower region.

"Okay, girlfriend, we've been off the ship and out of the Navy for a long time now. It's weird for you to use that term to describe that sensation."

There was no other way to describe it. It felt like an aroused adrenaline rush, the hairs on her arms and her moist panties were proof.

Patty gasped, inhaled, and exhaled.

"Oh…hot damn, I see the reason for your weird reaction. Four gorgeous men just sat in the lounge."

Cathryn turned to look in the direction Patty nodded and saw them. No, she saw *him*. Cathryn lost the ability to formulate a sentence. They were both awestruck then, together, said, "DAMN!"

The man who caught Cathryn's eye was gorgeous, which was an understatement. His hair jet black, cut in a professional style. His skin tanned, but his body ripped with muscles upon muscles. The outlines of his muscles could be seen through his sports coat. And he stared directly at her with deep, emerald green eyes. She had to blink a couple of times because they looked like they glowed slightly.

She became acutely aware of everything around her. Goosebumps appeared on her arms, her eyesight sharpened. At this distance, she could almost see the heat radiating off of his body.

Her rational brain said, *'Don't look at him, he's complete trouble. He's a man. Ignore those irrational sensations. You're in control.'* Her wolf stood up, ears perked with her emotional brain saying, *'Shut…the…fuck…up! It's been a while!'* If her wolf could have, it would have stood on its hind legs, front paws in the air, and yelled, *'New Chew Toy. He's MINE!'*

Chapter 3

Cathryn took a deep breath, picked up her tray, and walked up the small stairway to start her rounds through the lounge. She tried her best to ignore the gorgeous man who continued to stare at her. Nonchalantly Cathryn smiled, told the breathtaking gentlemen she'd be with them shortly, then proceeded to the back of the lounge. Time slowed as she walked back toward him. The eye contact with him intensified as her senses kicked up a couple of notches like an Emeril Lagasse BAM!

She momentarily broke eye contact with him as she approached their table. She started to speak, when her words caught in her throat. She cleared her throat and tried again.

"Good evening gentlemen, what would you like to have?"

The gentleman who stared at her raised his right eyebrow, then smiled. She realized she asked a loaded question, smiled wide, then whispered to herself, "Way to go, girl." They all laughed, they must have heard her private scolding. They each ordered a beer, except the man who continued to stare at her. His eyes were intense, focused, and practically held her in a trance.

'They are so green. I've never seen anyone with such an intense color green before.'

Which made her wolf answer, *'DUH!'*

She recovered from the hold he had on her.

"Sir, what would you like to drink?"

A gentleman to his left backhanded his arm.

"Answer the lady!"

"Huh? Oh...Um...Yes, beer, I would like a beer please." Oh, his voice, a low rumble, the sound was sexy and as smooth as cognac. The vibrations sent an electrical charge through her that settled in her southern region. Great goddess, his scent was enticing. Not like regular men's cologne, something different, alluring. Her breath caught in her throat and her heart skipped a couple of beats when he smiled at her. This was a first in a long, long time. Her shifter senses increased hard and fast while still in human form. A little dizziness overtook her as she walked back toward the cocktail station. She held on to the handrail as she walked down the steps, to keep her balance.

A loud commotion came from the High-Limit slot area. Someone released a blood-curdling scream as three security officers ran there. Patty walked back toward the station fast with a look of complete satisfaction on her face. There was broken glass all over her tray and the front of her uniform was wet.

"Are you okay?"

Cathryn leaned in close and whispered jokingly, "What did you do? Did you shift? I thought you were against shifting in public."

Patty looked her best friend in the eye with a look of innocence. Well, she tried to give her an innocent look but failed miserably. In a low, demure voice she said, "I did not shift. However, the shit-faced asshole in High-Limit slots won't be able to grab anyone's tail again. At least not for a while." She blinked innocently.

Patty shared that somehow his pinky and ring finger on his right hand got bent back toward the back of his hand. Having a spirit animal made shifters stronger and faster than other humans, even in human form. Patty asked Nick, the bartender, to call Roger and let him know she had to go to security to make a statement about the incident.

The casino and lounge weren't that busy considering it was Friday evening, but Nick took far too long to bring her drink orders back to her. She straightened out stir sticks, wrapped foam around coffee glasses, and cleaned her tray to keep busy.

She made eye contact every time she looked up at the gorgeous man with the amazing green eyes. She couldn't keep a stupid, cheesy grin off her face as the heat in her cheeks increased each time. She picked up a glass to wrap it in foam and stopped when she felt something. A low vibration which started in her mid-section, deep inside her being that spread throughout her body. As the vibration increased, it turned into a growl. She looked up again and realized it came from him. Slowly her world faded away. The music from the casino's speakers, noise from the slot machines, the table game players, crowds of patrons, and employees' conversations slowly disappeared.

She only felt and heard his growl. It called to her, beckoned her. Her breathing became shallow. She felt a sheen of perspiration form on her brow and cleavage. She heard a heartbeat, his heartbeat. It kept in rhythm with hers. Her wolf perked up again, she responded to him, compelled to react as if she had no other choice. His mating call pulled her, and his eyes responded with a slight glow.

Cathryn's reality returned when Nick stepped up with the four beers and other drinks. The casino's noise level returned. She almost couldn't remember what she was supposed to do, then slowly, realization returned. The light-headed dizzy feeling returned as she walked toward the four men. Her body heat increased the closer she approached him.

"Here you go, gentlemen."

They each tipped her.

"Thank you, I'll be back around soon, please let me know if there is anything else you need."

Before she walked off, she and the gorgeous man made eye contact again. She watched his eyes glance at her name tag pinned across her left breast.

"Cathryn? Yes, there is something else I would like. Your phone number."

"Oh, that's cute, like I haven't heard that line before. Seriously, if you gentlemen need another round, please let me know when I come back around."

He began to speak and put on the most dazzling smile she had ever seen. Beautiful, sensual lips that should be illegal.

"Oh, beautiful, I am dead serious. Can I get your number?"

"I'm sorry, but no. I have other guests to attend to. But I'll be back around."

"Yes, Cathryn…you do that."

Cathryn dropped off drinks to the other patrons in the lounge. As she walked back to the bar she turned and caught him staring again. She enjoyed the way her name fell from his lips.

Oh, my goddess!

She nearly dove into his lap to devour his lips when her name rolled off his tongue. It was so simple, yet so exciting. The hypnotic ring of his voice captured her and kept her from breathing.

***

Jake adjusted himself as he watched her walk toward the station.

"That's definitely an ass to nibble on." This time he said it out loud.

When she asked, 'what would you like to have?' he didn't think his cock could get any harder. His first thought of what he wanted. Her on her back under him, on her knees, his face between her thighs as she moaned, no, screamed his name.

He liked her response when he asked for her number. Her scent increased which was intoxicating, like nothing he ever encountered before. Her eyes dilated, her heartbeat increased. From that moment he knew she would be his. But she wanted to play hard to get. He always enjoyed a good hunt.

"Earth to Jake," Alex snapped his fingers in front of Jake's ear. "You have that look, brother. Are you going hunting?"

"Oh…yeah!" He turned back toward his friends.

"You going to tell her that you own half the casino?" Robert asked.

"No, I want her to want me for me, not my money. I bragged before and almost lost everything. Remember?"

"Yes, but your last girlfriend wasn't one of us. This Cathryn is. I can smell shifter all over her. And you know I never liked your last girlfriend, she fucking reeked of greed. Your uncle and I tried to tell you, but you wouldn't listen until it was almost too late," RL added.

Jake remembered his time with what's her name all too well. Fifteen years ago his sense of smell and instincts were entirely off. Since he was finally being honest with himself, he chose to ignore them. He was so pissed off at the world that even his wolf retreated from him.

His self-imposed celibacy might have just paid off, which would have driven any normal shifter crazy. For five years he waited for the right one to come into his life. His instincts believed this Cathryn might be the one. He knew what he had to do, strike at the right moment. He had to have Cathryn's full, undivided attention. This called for patience; hunting always called for patience.

First thing in the morning he would go see his Uncle Jonathan. In the meantime, he had some stalking to do. Not the 'I'm crazy' kind of stalking, but the 'oh so subtle I want to get to know you' kind. As for now, he enjoyed the view.

***

Cathryn made extra rounds through her assigned areas to distract her from the gorgeous man with the fabulous green eyes. Her senses finally dialed back, and she was able to focus on her job. But the distractions didn't last as long as Cathryn hoped. She imagined his lips all over her body. The sensual way he spoke her name damn near brought her to orgasm right then. Damn, he'd been brazen when he asked her for her number, completely sure of himself. Unlike what's his name. That arrogant, rude and, worst of all, controlling asshole. If she got to know him, would he be intimidated by her strength and independence?

What's his name had a problem with her independence. For the short time they dated, he had to make all the decisions. He tried to tell her what to do, where to go, and dictate all aspects of her life including their sexual activities. Her instincts told her he was not a good person, but for a short time she ignored the warning signs until it was almost too late. In hindsight, she should have paid attention to her dogs.

She dated a few guys since their breakup but couldn't connect with any of them. They didn't understand her. Some men didn't get fiercely independent women. She wanted a man who would hear her wants and needs. Someone secure enough in his manhood to let her be herself without trying to change her. Was that too much to ask for?

Mr. Emerald Eyes was intense. She felt his power, his dominance. He seemed very sure of himself, not because of the fact he asked for her number. She'd heard that same line hundreds of times. It always came from guys who were either shit-faced or just lecherous. Not this one, his hypnotic eyes and voice aroused her in ways no man ever had. As far back as she could remember her senses had never been as sharp as they were now.

She felt his presence from a slot area opposite the lounge. As she picked up empty glasses from the slot machines, a thought hit her.

'He's one of us, an empathic shifter. Where has he been all this time?'

She finished her last rounds through the lounge and asked the four gentlemen if they needed anything else. The all said no, so she called it a night.

Cathryn exchanged her small currency and table game chips for larger cash at the cashier's cage. She had to walk past the lounge toward the dressing room and involuntarily looked up at Mr. Emerald eyes as she passed. She watched his eyes follow her, but before she could catch herself, she inadvertently waved at him. He saluted her with his beer bottle, as an arousing chill spread throughout her body.

In the employee dressing room, she changed into her jeans, V-neck t-shirt, and hiking boots. She shouldered her purse, picked up her garment bag when Patty walked in, not looking too happy with her garment bag.

"Hey."

"Hey."

"What happened after you made your statement to security?"

Patty explained Roger went on a rant; he said she shouldn't attack the customers. She was to move out of that guy's way, and if that didn't work to call security.

“He sent me home early. I’m going on my date early. So, don’t wait up.”

“Well, I’m out of here. Have fun, be careful. See you when you get home and call if you need anything.”

On her way to the parking garage, Cathryn remembered she left her lip gloss at the lounge bar station. When she arrived, she felt a hint of disappointment because the gorgeous man with the green eyes was no longer there. Nick, the bartender, handed her a piece of paper as she stepped up to the bar.

“I swear there is something familiar about that big guy.”

She took the note from Nick.

“What big guy?”

“The one with the intense green eyes. The one who stared at you all night? I just can’t place where I’ve seen him before.”

Cathryn looked at the piece of paper.

“What’s this?”

“He said to give this to you.”

Cathryn opened the paper and frowned. *‘Turn around’* was written on the paper.

Turn around? What the hell does that mean?

A tingling sensation washed over her again. She didn’t need to turn around to know he was there. Slowly she turned, and there he was, three feet away, leaning against a slot machine. He greeted her with his brilliant smile, which should be illegal in all fifty states, Canada, and Mexico. How the hell did he know she would return to the lounge bar?

He stepped closer.

"Hi; it just dawned on me I know your name, but you don't know mine. I wouldn't be a gentleman if I left knowing you didn't have a name to put to the face you'll be dreaming of tonight. My name is Jake."

He winked then put his hand out to her. She grasped his hand, and her brain screamed 'Hot Damn' as an electrical charge ran from his hand straight to her pussy.

The energy and heat flowing into her was intense. Then, in slow motion, he brought her hand to his lips and kissed it. It wasn't one of those quick I'm pretending to be a perfect gentleman, pecks. This was slow. Deliberate, with full lips caressing her knuckles. Her lips parted slightly as a euphoric breath passed them. Her knees were close to buckling as a mental fog washed over her. No man had ever kissed her hand before, let alone with such declaration.

She stood there, completely enthralled by his features. His hair was thick, shiny, and wavy like the waves of the ocean at night. Visions flashed through her mind of her fisting handfuls of them while his lips and tongue did wonderfully delicious things between her legs.

She studied his beautiful eyes again. Hints of aqua flecks outlined the emerald color. He had sharp features, medium cheekbones, chiseled chin, and dimples in his cheeks when he smiled. A dusting of five o'clock shadow completed his rugged handsomeness.

Cathryn uncontrollably caressed his cheek with her little finger as he kissed her hand. The softness of his skin and facial hair sent another wave of sensations along her nerve endings. He was the sexiest man she had ever seen. She hadn't realized how heavy her breathing became until her attention was brought back to her hand as he drew circles on the back with his thumb.

She gave him her undivided attention. There wasn't anything else on her mind except him. Cathryn stood there rigid, mesmerized by his features as if she needed to memorize them. She licked her bottom lip. His eyes darted to her lips then back to her eyes again. Cathryn felt his arousal. His heat surrounded her. Cathryn felt warm and protected. At that very moment, she knew he wanted her just as much as she wanted him.

"I hope I get to see you again soon. I would hate to think this would be our first and only meeting."

Cathryn finally exhaled the breath she hadn't realized she held and became aware of her surroundings again.

"Hmm, oh, you probably will, if you plan on returning here. However, this is my weekend, so for the next two days I will be free of this place."

"You're most definitely my favorite cocktail waitress here, so I'll have to come back."

Then, just as deliberate and as reverent as before, he kissed her hand again. Before she could stop herself, a sensual moan slipped between her lips, and she creamed her jeans.

Jake stepped back from her. She watched his nostrils flare and inhale. He raised he eyebrow. He smiled as his eyes licked her from her eyes to her toes then back up to her eyes again. He stepped closer, leaned in, then pressed his lips close to her ear.

"By the way, you look remarkable in fur."

He slowly released her hand and walked away.

Cathryn leaned against the slot machine and slowly lowered herself. Good thing there was a chair there, or her butt would have hit the floor. Slowly she rose to her feet as she very slowly took in deep breaths. The breathing part was a little hard as she watched him walk away. The man's walk was even sexy. He carried his shoulders and back straight like a predator. People moved out of his way as he walked.

She took in another breath then slowly released it through her lips in an 'o' shape. She started to walk toward the employee exit when she remembered why she came back to the lounge bar: her lip gloss.

"Nick, how did he know I would come back to the lounge?"

"He must have overheard me say you left your lipstick here and assumed you would return. He gave me the note and then you returned."

Chapter 4

The drive home, all Jake thought about was the beautiful woman he met. Her eyes, the most striking deep amber he'd ever seen and the way she looked up at him with such intensity. Her voluptuous lips begged him to taste. To take them long, deep, and passionately. When her tongue snaked out to lick her bottom lip, his cock became the consistency of mahogany. He loved the way she carried herself, the sway of her hips smooth and graceful. She looked like she worked out but still had soft curves. Jake had a feeling her round breasts would fit perfectly in his big hands. He fantasized how her toned, voluptuous legs would feel wrapped around his waist as he drove deep into her hot, wet pussy.

All he knew about this beautiful woman was her first name: Cathryn. "Cathryn." His jeans tightened more when he said her name aloud. First thing in the morning he would call his uncle to chat. Talk about the hunt with the boys, and then ask about her. Two days, he wouldn't see her for two whole days. Nerve-wracking, but he was patient.

Jake's cell beeped a winter storm warning from the west. He needed to make sure all the windows and fences were secured as soon as he arrived home.

Snow began to fall when he arrived at the cabin. The wind blew about fifteen miles an hour. His cabin was built by his grandfather over sixty years ago, on prime Mt. Charleston land. Back then it was only a large one-room cabin, which he left to his only grandson.

As Jake stepped out of his truck a strong gust of wind pushed him into his truck door. He heard an ethereal voice louder than before and more evident: *"She's closer now."*

He turned around, but there was no one there. The voice definitely sounded like his grandfather. Jake shook his head, shrugged his shoulders, then continued into the cabin.

A chill hit him when he entered. The cabin felt much colder inside. He kept his jacket on as he switched on the lights. He could see his breath billow and he went directly to the fireplace. He raked the embers slightly as their glow erupted from the dark ashes, grabbing a few logs from the stack beside the fireplace. The warmth of the fire began to radiate throughout the room.

The great room was the original one room of the cabin when his grandfather owned it. Jake had since remodeled it upon his separation from the Corps. He added more space on the ground floor and a second level.

The warm blaze took the chill of the great room. Jake squatted down in front to warm his hands then proceeded back outside. After he checked the fences, shutters, and the barn to make sure everything was secure, Jake checked the windows and water heater. He made sure the propane tanks were working. It would suck to start the next morning with a cold shower.

That tingling sensation wove through his body, and the face of the beautiful woman took center stage in his mind again. More thoughts ran around in his mind.

'What is she doing now? Did she make it home safely? Wherever home was.'

Strange how protective he felt over her suddenly. He was home safe, but his big house was very, very empty. Hopefully not for long. There seemed to be light at the end of that dark and lonely tunnel. This time he hoped it wasn't a train.

***

As Cathryn turned into her driveway, there was a half inch of snow on the ground. Her four fur babies immediately ran toward the gate. They jumped all around her, waiting for her attention. They'd missed their mommy. She knelt down and greeted each with a hug. She hadn't worried too much about them being outside all day; they were bred for this kind of weather.

As she led them toward the cabin, a gust of wind rushed her and knocked her into the front door.

"Trust him" came an ethereal voice as the sharp wind cut through her. She turned, looked around, but saw nothing and no one. Weird, how that voice almost sounded like her Nana.

She immediately felt the chilled air as she entered with the dogs behind her. Thank the goddess she remembered to put wood next to the fireplace before she and Patty went to work. She lit the fire then proceeded to get the dogs their food.

The cabin she shared with Patty was 3,000-square-feet, with two levels. Her Nana had it built back when she was in high school. Two master bedrooms upstairs with full baths and two offices downstairs. The living room contained a sunken square pit couch with cushions all around. A big flat screen TV was attached to the wall above the fireplace.

Now and then Cathryn could smell her Nana's scent in the room. It brought back memories of her time here on the mountain. Nana, her father's mother, was of Native American descent, from the local Paiute tribe. Nana instilled in her all the legends and teachings of her shape-shifting abilities. She taught her about nature, flora, and fauna. Nana reminded her to respect the environment and remember that they too were part of life. Daily meditations were mandatory, to not only connect with her spirit animal but to control her spirit animal as well. Synergy had to be achieved by both. Sometimes Patty joined them on the weekends to learn the cool magick of being a shifter.

Nana retired from the Bureau of Indian Affairs after Cathryn graduated from high school, sold the house in the city, and moved them up to the mountain.

Cathryn felt tired, yet not enough to go to bed. She fed the dogs, grabbed a bottle of Captain Morgan's Spiced rum with a bottle of Dr. Pepper with a glass of ice, then proceeded to the living room. A movie was in order, something to relax her after a long day hustling drinks to others.

She placed the bottles and glass on the coffee table then searched her DVD library. Something action-packed; no mushy love story for her tonight. After meeting Jake and the two steamy kisses he gave her, that was enough to keep her antsy all weekend. She still felt the heat from his lips on her hands. Just the thought of his name made her body shiver with sensations that caused her to hyperventilate. So, action movie it is, blood, guts, and death, yeah that sounded better.

She found the perfect movie. Inserted the disk into the Blu-Ray player then plopped back down on the couch. She grabbed her glass, poured her drink, took a sip, then swallowed.

"Aaahh, that's good."

Her nerves and muscles began to relax as the battle cry from the Spartan King echoed through the room.

***

Jake felt exhausted from his day. He decided to rest in his bedroom with a movie. Jake needed to take his mind off Cathryn. He searched through his DVD collection; he wanted something with lots of action, no sex scenes, okay maybe just one. Out of his choices of various action movies, he couldn't find anything that grabbed his attention, until…Ah ha, the perfect choice. Yes, multiple battles, lots of blood and gore. Just what he needed to relax and take his mind off her.

Jake grabbed a couple of beers from his kitchen, walked back to his bedroom, and popped the disc into the player. He propped pillows behind him and relaxed against his headboard as the wind howled outside. Jake took a long swallow, closed his eyes, and moaned as the cold liquid slid down his throat. He finally began to relax; between the hunt this morning and meeting the perfect woman tonight, he was asleep before he knew it. The last thing he heard was the battle cry of King Leonidas to the Spartan Army.

Chapter 5

Moonlight spilled through the balcony doorway; white linens billowed in the breeze that hung from the walls all around him. He lay in a massive bed that didn't feel like his. White satin sheets covered his lower body; he felt perspiration on his skin as he lay there with his eyes closed. He wasn't asleep but not fully awake either. A voice called his name,

"Jake."

That was a woman's voice. But it sounded far away and ethereal; he stirred but could not open his eyes. She called his name again.

"Jake." This time it was louder.

He gasped, opened his eyes, then raised his head. A vision of beauty slowly walked toward him. There was just enough light that he could only see her silhouette in the shadows, but he could tell how beautiful she was. He could only see the outline of her facial features. But her eyes, they glowed a deep amber color; her hair was curly, dark, and just long enough to brush past her shoulders. She was draped in a sheer, gauzy white toga gown that gathered at her left shoulder and showed her full, round breasts.

She continued to call his name as she stepped to the foot of the massive bed. Slowly she raised her gown and kneeled on the bed. She crawled toward him, like a predator stalking her prey, and he was her prey. She stopped between his legs and bent her head low, then nuzzled his crotch. A wicked grin spread on her face. He was aroused, and she could smell his arousal.

Slowly she pulled the satin sheet down and revealed his cock. She bent low to nuzzle and sniff him again from his base to his mushroom head, which responded instantly to this woman and curved toward his belly. His breath rapidly invaded and escaped his lungs to the point of hyperventilating.

She placed her hand on his cock with her elbows on either side of his hips, then bent her face toward his cock and licked him from the base up.

He sucked air in through gritted teeth, then pressed his head back into the pillow and moaned. When he raised his head again, he watched her as she slowly, meticulously assaulted his cock with her mouth and tongue. She licked him, sucked him up then down. She made sure every inch of his cock was attended to. She shifted her weight to her left, wrapped her right hand around the base of his cock, and gently massaged him. Leisurely, she brought him to her lips, licked tight circles, and left tiny kisses on his mushroom head. Pre-cum formed in the seam as she licked again. He began panting as she kissed him then opened her mouth to suck him slowly in. She massaged up and down his shaft as she sucked with each pull. She pulled him deep into her mouth until she finally had most of his cock. She kept her rhythm slow with the motion then released him from her mouth while she massaged his shaft with her hand.

She glanced up at him as his hips moved to the same rhythm she stroked him. He looked down at her, his eyes locked onto her glowing amber ones. They were the most beautiful eyes he'd ever seen, but they seemed familiar. Her features were so attractive, and damn...she knew what she was doing to his cock. His head rolled back then pushed into the pillow as she engulfed his cock again. He rocked his hips harder as he pushed his cock deeper into her mouth and back out. He fisted his hands into her hair, just to feel if she was real. His breathing became a steady rough pant as he moaned in pleasure. She moaned around his cock and met his response, which vibrated through his cock.

He couldn't take anymore; he had to be inside her now. Gently he grabbed her by her shoulders and pulled her up to him. She straddled him; he placed his hands on her hips as she put her hands on his chest. In an instant, he impaled her as he gasped for air.

He couldn't move for what seemed like an eternity. She began to roll her hips and pushed down as he finally rolled his hips up. He pushed deep and hard as she met him thrust for thrust. A slow, steady rhythm quickly became faster and harder, with so much intensity he panted through gritted teeth. Before he climaxed, he pulled her onto the length of his body and rolled her onto her back. The light of the full moon spilled onto her face to reveal who she was. His breath caught as he looked down at her and saw her face for the first time.

"Cathryn?"

He looked into those deep amber eyes. Cathryn smiled and with a very seductive voice said, "Yes, my love."

She began to undulate under him, which was his invitation to thrust deep. He grabbed the back of her knees, spread her legs wide, then began to push harder and deeper. He never took his eyes off of hers as he rocked harder, deeper, and faster. He grunted his pleasure, and with every thrust she called his name again and again. His orgasm started like a small wave, but quickly built to a tsunami. The faster he rolled his hips, the bigger the wave felt and the more she screamed his name. As soon as the wave crested, his orgasm slammed into him with so much intensity, he growled, howled like his wolf, and collapsed on top of his dream lady.

***

Cathryn awoke face down in her bed, drenched in sweat and wetter between her legs then she'd ever been in her life. Her sheets twisted around her body as she rolled onto her back. Slowly, very slowly, Cathryn opened her eyes. She looked around to make sure she was still in her bedroom.

"Yep, still in my room."

As she tried to sit up, she felt soreness throughout her body. Her body felt like she'd been through a vigorous self-defense workout. Cathryn swung her legs around to the edge of the bed and moaned as her feet hit the floor. The ache could be felt as she wobbled into her bathroom. Cathryn turned on the shower, adjusted the temperature, then stepped under the spray. She placed her hands against the walls and leaned her head back as the water pressure pounded onto her scalp and shoulders. A moan escaped her when she turned her body under the spray as the heated water began to relax her muscles. She grabbed her loofah, poured shower gel onto it, and started to lather her arms then legs. Heat pooled in her core as she soaped her breasts. Then the vivid dream replayed in her mind…

She ran on all fours through a forest, covered in black fur. The moon was full, and the whole forest was bright with its glow. The scents of rosemary, pine, and sage drifted through her long muzzle. But there was also another scent, a male. He was hunting her, fast. The faster she ran, the faster he ran. Every directional change she made, he changed with her. It was as if he was in her head and knew which direction she would go. Soon he would close the distance between them.

He was hunting her, and she sensed it was not for food. This male wanted to mate. Now! She could smell his arousal. She wanted him just as much, but she wasn't going to make it easy for him. If he wanted her, he would have to work hard. As she ran, now and then she would turn her head behind to see just how close he was. She could see him now. He was huge, with black fur. Massive muscles rippled as he moved and closed the distance between them.

The forest became thicker, the moonlight through the trees thinned, but she still saw ahead of her. She broke through a patch of dense brush, into a clearing with low grass and flowers everywhere, just beyond lay a small pond. She slowed down long enough to sniff the air, to choose which direction to go. Something slammed into her, knocked the wind from her as she rolled onto her side. Quickly she stood and saw him. He was much larger than she had thought. She could feel his emotions. He was aroused, and he wanted her. He stalked toward her, as she backed away slowly.

She kept her eye contact with him, as they shifted in the same instant.

With the moon directly at his back, she couldn't see his face. The only facial features she saw were his glowing emerald green eyes. They were both naked. She gazed down his body and saw the shadowy outline of his muscles. His shoulders were broad; his massive chest heaved as he breathed heavily, his arm muscles bulged, his waist and hips narrow. Her eyes traveled downward, even more, his thighs were just as muscular but what she noticed was his cock. It was long, thick, and curved toward his navel. Her breathing increased as her nipples hardened and stood straight at him as an invitation. Moisture began to drip from between her legs, and she knew he could smell her arousal, just as she could. She backed away as he stepped towards her and asked,

"What do you want?"

His voice was low, husky almost a growl, "Isn't it obvious," as he stroked his cock.

" Well, I hope you don't think I'm that easy."

" Oh, no baby, you gave me a terrific run, but playtime is over, time to claim you and make you mine!"

"You want me?" she said with a grin. "Come and get me!"

He took two steps then leaped at her, but she ducked, rolled onto the ground, and landed in a crouched position. "You look hungry." She giggled and smiled. As she tried to anticipate his next move, he leaped toward her again. She moved to get out of his path, but she wasn't fast enough. He landed on her and rolled her onto her belly with him on her back.

He leaned in close and nuzzled her ear.

"My lady, you and I have unfinished business." He released a soft, low growl.

The vibrations set off a tingling sensation starting from her head and toes then shot straight into her pussy. He spread her arms on the ground above her as she lowered her head then rested her cheek on the grass. She panted from the heat that rushed throughout her body. He fisted his hand into hers then slowly spread her legs with his knees. She raised her hips slightly as she felt his rigid hard cock against her ass. He positioned the head of his cock at her pussy entrance then slid right in. As he pushed into her, her channel pulsated and pulled him in further as if it needed to hold on for dear life. She let out a small gasp when he nuzzled her neck then nipped her shoulder. He rolled his hips to push deep inside her. She released another gasp then raised her hips to match his thrusts.

He released her right hand and slowly caressed her arm, up past her shoulder then around to her breast. She raised her body up just a bit to give him more room. His hands were big, strong and smooth. When he rubbed her nipple side to side, her breathing became shallow, almost panting. He continued to move his hand down her body with unbearable slowness, past her ribs then around her belly. Wave after wave of intense electricity increased as she knew where those fingers were going and craved their touch.

She felt as if she was on the edge of a cliff when his fingers finally reached their destination, her clit. Unable to control her panting, she turned her head to the right, to finally see the man's face who lovingly teased her. She gasped and cried out, "Jake?"

"Hey, baby."

She smiled at him in response to his sexy smile as he rolled his hips, sliding in and out faster this time. She pushed her hips back into him, just as hard, and matched his rhythm.

She felt her orgasm swell like a rapid river's torrent, with each thrust. As the pressure built, he called her name with each thrust which picked up speed. She wanted this to last, but Jake had other plans. He pressed his lips close to her ear then released a low and commanding growl that sent her over the edge. She screamed her pleasure to him and the universe. He released her hands, fisted her hair then turned her face to him. He took her mouth with his and feasted on her as if he had not eaten in days. He reluctantly released her lips and rested his mouth against her neck without breaking his rhythm. He rocked harder into her and panted as if he still ran while he massaged her clit. Another orgasm was about to spill out of her when he growled again. The last thing she remembered him saying was, "MINE!" as he bit into her shoulder. Her climax slammed into her like a freight train barreling down a train track.

Chapter 6

Cathryn shut the water off, grabbed a fluffy bath sheet and wrapped it around her. As she stepped out of the shower, her legs still felt a little wobbly. Cathryn leaned on the sink with both hands on the edge and took a deep breath. She looked at the foggy mirror as she released it then wiped the condensation to check her shoulder. Nope, no mating marks.

"That dream felt too damn real."

She put on a pair of jeans, a sweatshirt, then went downstairs to let the dogs out. Everything outside was covered in white. The storm dropped at least a foot and a half of snow. After a few minutes the dogs scratched at the door; she started her breakfast after she fed them.

Her breakfast became cold as she sat at the table. Sometimes her dream replayed in her mind as she drifted off with her fork in her hand on the plate. She felt tingling sensations in certain parts of her anatomy as if she genuinely had had wild animal sex. This unnerved her and yet somehow excited her at the same time.

She finally finished her breakfast and walked to the sink and placed her dishes in the dishwasher. She looked out the window as a vehicle pulled into the driveway. Patty finally made it home from her date.

The gate slammed shut with a loud thud. The dogs greeted Patty at the door while she stomped the snow off her boots. She grumbled to herself as she tried to move around them.

"Hey!" Patty sounded extremely pissed.

"Soooo…how was your date?"

Cathryn already knew the answer. She didn't need to be empathic to see her best friend was pissed.

"Shitty!" she stomped past Cathryn, upstairs to her room, then slammed her door.

Cathryn heard her shower run and thought maybe she would cool down afterward. After so many years of being friends, close as sisters even, when one was in a lousy mood, and one-word responses were given, they gave each other space and time to calm down. Then the venting would begin.

Patty returned downstairs after her shower, made herself a cup of coffee and proceeded to the living room. Cathryn sat reading a book.

"Feel better?"

"Yes, a little."

"You ready to spill it?"

"Yes."

"What happened? Or, better yet, what didn't happen?"

"What didn't happen?"

Patty told Cathryn the story of her disastrous date. From the time she left work, to when she met her date at the restaurant. Which went downhill from there. How the night became progressively worse through dinner.

"That man couldn't eat, let alone fuck his way out of a wet paper bag."

"Wow, okay. Well, you obviously need to work off some of that pent-up sexual tension. Do you want to go for a run with me tonight?"

"No. The mood I'm in, my wolf might take control, and I could kill something or someone."

Cathryn's own sexual tension was at an all-time high. Her self-imposed celibacy was not going as well as she had hoped. And her wolf was not helping at all. Her wolf liked Jake's scent and wanted to play with him and his wolf.

A good run with her wild side was what she needed. At least she hoped so. The fact she has not gotten laid in a while had not helped either. Her dream replayed again front and center which had her in a constant state of arousal.

***

Jake felt antsy since he woke this morning tangled in his sheets, a pool of sticky body fluids and sweat. He paced in the great room of his uncle's palatial estate. He was so distracted he forgot to take off his denim jacket. His dream of her magnificent body and the way she gave him head kept him with a perpetual hard-on all day. Because that dream felt eerily too real.

Chapter 7

Uncle Jonathan was a slightly more mature-looking version of Jake, despite the slight gray at his temples. When people saw them together in public, they asked if they were brothers. Of course, Jonathan being the cocky alpha, loved seeing their surprised looks when he or Jake told them no. He often said not too bad for someone in his mid-50s. He was also a very, very powerful empathic shifter.

Jonathan wasn't too surprised to see his nephew. Jake usually stopped by about twice a week. But, this was the third time this week. Something was up; Jonathan could feel it and smell it all over him.

Jonathan embraced his nephew with a hug and a slap on the back.

"So, son, what brings you to my humble home today?" Jonathan closed his eyes, inhaled deep, relaxed then exhaled. "Better yet. What's her name?" he sensed the truth.

Jonathan loved the surprised look Jake always got when he got straight to the point of any situation.

"What do you mean? I just came by to say hey, and to see what you were up to."

Jonathan slowly sat down in his leather recliner, eased it back; he never took his eyes off of his nephew.

"I smell bullshit, boy. I'm going to ask you again…what…is…her…name?"

Jonathan used his command alpha tone. He only used that tone when Jake tried to avoid telling him the straight truth. He also knew it made Jake feel like he was eight years old again and was caught doing something he wasn't supposed to be doing. Jonathan watched Jake swallow, take a deep breath then exhale. Jake finally took off his jacket and sat down on the sofa across from him.

"Her name's Cathryn, and she's a cocktail waitress at the casino."

Jonathan listened as Jake told him his story. The more he spoke, the more Jake's scent poured off him. Jake also shared he felt Cathryn was one of them, a shifter that he felt sure of it.

"We'll discuss this more over lunch, son."

Jonathan needed to see where his nephew's head was at with this new one. He remembered Jake's rebellious side all too well, which started after the death of Jake's parents when he was ten. The family was devastated when the news came about his brother's accident. He and five other Marines died when their helicopter went down on a training mission in the desert. Of course, they all felt the void, but it seemed to be worst for Jake's mother.

Jonathan and his brother were very close. He still missed him to this day. He tried to set aside his pain to help his sister-in-law and nephew, but nothing helped. Jake's emotions were all over the place. His poor sister-in-law sank into a severe depression, to the point she became unable to take care of herself let alone a ten-year-old. Eventually, she took her own life later that same year.

Jake's teenage years were the worst six years of Jonathan's life. There were times he literally wanted to murder his nephew. The boy seemed to purposely piss him and his grandfather off. Jonathan felt and understood why Jake acted out, but that still did not stop the fact that he wanted on numerous occasions to bury his nephew alive.

The girls Jake dated left much to be desired. Especially the one fifteen years ago. There were arguments over them all, but the argument over that last one almost became physical. He needed to see where Jake's head was at with this new woman.

***

Cathryn's body still tingled from her hot dream the night before. Dressed in jeans, t-shirt, hiking boots, she pulled on her black leather fur-lined coat then stepped out the front door. The chilly evening air felt great against her hot skin. The full moonlight sparkled off the snow. Snow lined the naked tree branches.

Patty was still a little upset from her disastrous date, so Cathryn gave her some space. As she walked out the door, the dogs greeted her with their usual enthusiasm. The played, jumped and romped all around her as Cathryn headed toward the metal fence. When she reached the fence, they stopped. They understood what was to come, laid down, and waited silently.

She looked around, sniffed the air to make sure no one was around. She closed her eyes, called her magick then visualized her wolf. In less than a moment, she shifted and was on all fours. She turned her body to look at herself. Her black fur shined in the moonlight; she raised her muzzle, shook her body to fluff out her fur. She flipped her tail, jumped and cleared the fence then took off toward the south.

She didn't know why that direction, but her instincts told her to go that way, so she went. She heard the ethereal voice again, and again it sounded like her Nana's voice.

"He's that way. Go to him."

***

Lunch turned into dinner with his uncle. Besides the talk about Cathryn, Jake told his uncle about the hunt with the boys. Jonathan shared the latest financial information on the casino. Most of his tension faded away from him the more he spent with his uncle.

He looked at the background check records the casino had done on her before she was hired. He knew her last name now. Her family had been in the southwest for a long, long time. At least three generations African American on her mother's side; she was half Native American on her dad's side. That combination explained her exotic skin color, which he found beautiful. He couldn't wait to learn more about her.

Jake all of a sudden felt hyper. His adrenaline increased as he turned into his driveway. That tingling sensation returned as soon as he stepped out of his truck. A small gust of wind blew across his skin and spoke to him again. *"She's on her way, pup; be ready and be patient."* He turned around and again didn't see anyone. The ethereal voice was clearer this time and did have his grandfather's voice. His instincts told him to shift. He called his magick, visualized his wolf. *"Go north, pup."* He didn't question his instincts and headed toward the north.

It had been a while since he'd shifted. He loved this time with his wolf, the balance of logic and emotion. He felt exhilarated, finally able to stretch his legs. It had been too long since his last run. Sometimes he stopped and sniffed the ground to see who or what had been through his territory. Now and then he raised his muzzle to smell the air to get his bearings. He turned his body around, with his muzzle high. He inhaled a scent on the wind which came from the north. He recognized that scent. It was strong as the wind continued to carry it toward him. He tasted it, and his cock hardened. About five miles from the north, it was her! His heart raced with anticipation, which had nothing to do with his increased speed. Exciting was an understatement, that scent belonged to her, and she headed in his direction. Questions raced through his mind as fast as he ran.

'What was she doing out here? Does she know about him? Would she care about him and not his money?'

***

Cathryn was so engrossed in her run she hadn't realized how far she'd gone. She'd sometimes stop and sniffed a bush, marked other shrubs and various trees. Cathryn startled rabbits and other little creatures into flight. Chased a deer for about a half mile just because she could.

The wind suddenly changed, and a mist formed. Cathryn stopped dead in her tracks, sniffed, but all she picked up was the forest and animals. Then there was a scent, something very familiar. The mist became thicker, very recognizable. It looked almost like her grandmother. Cathryn shifted and started to panic as the fog became practically a solid form. The mist was her Nana! But that was impossible; she died almost two years ago to the day.

Then the mist spoke.

"Hello, baby girl."

Cathryn stood there shocked and amazed. Her panic almost became a full-blown freak-out when her Nana spoke again.

"It's okay, it's me. Remember I told you that I would come to you when you needed me?"

Cathryn's mouth hung wide open.

"Uh-huh…"

Her chest heaved as chilled air billowed out her mouth. She finally composed herself and remembered Nana's teaching about spirit guides. Messengers who came in times of need. She relaxed a little but was still confused.

"But Nan, I'm fine. I don't need anything. Really, I'm okay."

Mist Nana's expression changed to a scowl.

"Yes, you do. You have stopped trusting men. You have stopped trusting yourself to make the right decision because of the bad decisions you have made in the past. You have denied yourself physical contact because you think they are all alike."

Before Cathryn could protest, Nana's spirit began to fade.

"We all make mistakes; I have told you before, learn from them. Live life and have fun. And please, child, stop hiding on the damn mountain."

Nana was gone. Cathryn stood there with her mouth still wide open.

"Wow," she whispered.

She'd just received an ass-chewing from hell. Well, maybe not literally from hell. Literally from the grave, though, but still, that was an ass-chewing.

Shocked by what just transpired she felt that tingling sensation again. Then she heard the snap of a twig behind her. She turned; her eyes grew wide as her jaw dropped to her chest. There in front of her stood the biggest black timber wolf she'd ever seen. The massive beast stood about five feet away from her. She'd seen the wolves at the sanctuary behind the casino, but their size was nothing compared to the one in front of her now. She'd been so distracted by Nana's appearance, she hadn't sensed or felt anything until the wolf was almost upon her.

The height of its head reached her chest, its shoulders broad. But its eyes were different. Not the typical yellow, they were a deep emerald green. Like the ones from her dream. She stood perfectly still as the wolf slowly stalked toward her. Her heart raced fast; she felt it would burst through her chest. Her breathing became panting to the point of panic.

Heavy puffs of air escaped it muzzle like a chimney. It stopped its approach when it reached Cathryn's feet. It lowered its head and sniffed at her boots. She heard its deep inhales as its head moved up her legs. She felt emotions from somewhere but was too panicked to look around; she didn't know who or where the feelings came from. She felt curiosity, joy, and lust.

The tingling wave she felt before caressed her body as the wolf moved its head up her legs. The emotions that came caused wetness to form in her panties. When the wolf reached the junction between her legs, she watched its nostrils flair as it tried to push its muzzle in between her legs. A moan escaped her lips; she gasped and stepped back.

The wolf never backed up. It shifted into a man. Into *the* man. The tall, gorgeous man from the lounge. She looked up at him, then down and back up again. He was dressed in hiking boots, jeans, a knit turtleneck sweater and a fleece-lined denim jacket. She took in his broad shoulders, full chest, narrow waist and thick thighs. She definitely liked what she saw.

She gasped, "You!"

"Yes…"

"What are you doing here?"

"I live around here, about five miles south. What are you doing here?"

"I live in that direction."

She pointed toward the north. "I guess about ten miles. You can shift? Into a wolf?"

"Yes, I can. And I see you can, too!"

"Oh yeah? What makes you think that?"

She watched his eyes roam from her eyes to her feet then back up again as he stalked toward her. He bent his head toward her and sniffed.

"Well, for one, I can smell you."

'How can a man sniffing her make her flood her panties?'

He raised his head then looked into her eyes.

"And two, you just said you live about ten miles in that direction. We are in the middle of the thick forest, and I don't think you would want to be on a hike out here in this weather at this time of night. Unless you're a wolf."

His closeness felt very enjoyable, like something she'd needed for a very long time. Her breath hitched as he reached into her coat for her waist. He pulled her close to him. He was so tall she had to lean back to look at his face.

Her instincts let her know it was okay to touch him. Slowly she moved her hands up his arms to his biceps. She felt him flex as she touched him, and he smiled. She moved closer to him as he slowly lowered his face toward hers. Their lips met halfway as his caressed her. The sensation shocked her; she gasped as he slid his tongue over her lips. When she opened her mouth to breathe his tongue slipped past her lips and over her tongue. She moaned as his kiss became ravenous and her senses exploded.

The more she moaned, the more passionate his kiss became. Their tongues danced together in a rhythm as if they were made to do so. She felt surrounded by his heat as his hands caressed up her back, down her waist to her hips, and cupped her ass. He pulled her close as he rocked against her with his hard bulge. She felt his power, his dominance and his promise to possess all of her.

Cathryn gripped handfuls of his jacket. She needed to get closer to him, his body and his tongue. Cathryn stood on tiptoes, wrapped her arms around his neck then lost herself in his arms, his lips and his touch. Cathryn's breathing became shallow as she panted into his mouth. She was amazed how skilled this man kissed and quickly dismissed any thought of if any man had ever kissed her this thoroughly before.

She realized they stood there for what seemed like an eternity, but only a few moments passed. When Jake raised his head, she released a moan of protest and gazed into the most fabulous green eyes she'd ever seen. She was dazed and almost speechless for the first time in her life when he asked her a question.

"My lady, please come home with me?"

The timbre of his voice plucked at her nerve endings and made her shiver with excitement.

Cathryn's logical mind response would have been a resounding. No! She knew nothing about this man, only his name, and his first name at that. She just found out where he lived, he was her neighbor, although they were about fifteen miles apart but still her neighbor. Now she stood in the middle of the forest on the side of a mountain, almost a dozen miles from home, with a man she just met not twenty-four hours before. She said what any good red-blooded American woman would say.

"Yes."

Mainly, now that she had her Nana's permission to have fun. The heat she felt roll off of him could have melted a glacier. And his smile lit up the night sky, melting her panties.

"So, five miles; how long do you think it will take us to get there?"

She didn't think that smile could get any more charming.

"Not long if we run on all fours."

They shifted at the same time. Jake and Cathryn looked at each other as if they needed to memorize how each other looked. Cathryn stood still and watched as he circled her. Her brain shut down when Jake sniffed her. For a split second, she thought he was going to mount her, and she would have let him because his scent was intoxicating. He took the lead toward his house, and she was right on his tail.

'He looks just like the wolf from my dream. Big, beautiful and powerful.'

Chapter 8

They shifted together when they reached his cabin. Cathryn was amazed how big his cabin looked from the outside. It was almost twice the size of hers. This wasn't a cabin, it was a house in the woods.

He took her coat once inside and offered her a seat. Although the size had her in awe, the interior design was not a surprise to her in the least. It was strictly male. There were deer heads mounted on the walls. A large gun cabinet stood against the right wall and another one with bows and arrows next to that one. What else would a man living on a mountain have? A large fireplace stood in the corner of the room. A massive flat screen TV sat just to the right of the fireplace. A seven-foot-long black letter buttoned sofa with four ottomans dominated the center of the room.

"What would you like to drink?"

"Anything will be fine, thanks."

She'd been admiring some of his wall hangings when that tingling sensation wove up through her body. She felt him approach behind her but never heard his footfalls. When she turned, she was suddenly nose to his chest. He carried a bottle of wine with two wine glasses. His scent surrounded her, musk and deep forest. Cathryn never had any man have this kind of effect on her before. She felt overwhelmed; she tried to remain in control, so she took a deep, deep breath. But that didn't help, his scent crept into her cells, and Cathryn lost the last bit of her control. She looked up into his eyes; she couldn't resist his pull anymore. Cathryn caressed her hands up his six-pack, to his chest. She felt his arms encircle her waist as her arms moved up and around his neck. Cathryn wove her fingers into his hair as he lowered his lips to hers. She moaned as their tongues danced and played together. She heard a clink then his hands caressed up and down her back, his hands moved lower to caress then massage her ass. Cathryn moaned a deep vibration against his lips, as he continued to stroke her firm globes. He continued to move his hands down further; temporarily he broke their kiss and told her "Hold on."

Jake grabbed her legs, picked her up then resumed their kiss. Cathryn immediately wrapped her legs around his waist as she felt him walk somewhere. She didn't know or care as long as he kept his lips locked on hers. He must have stopped walking because he leaned her back then said, "Don't let go."

He crawled to the middle of the bed on his knees, and then slowly laid her down with him on top. His kiss became passionate as if he would die if she let her lips leave his. He rocked his hips side to side; his bulge increased in his jeans as he rubbed against her pussy. With every roll of his hips, a wave caressed her skin as her breathing increased.

"Oh baby, I need you naked," he whispered against her lips between kisses.

Cathryn panted, her brain would not let her mouth produce any coherent speech. She simply nodded yes. Jake moved off of her. As she started to untie her boots, he stopped her hands.

"Wait, let me do this. I've been dreaming about doing this all day."

He wanted to undress her. Cathryn was in awe that he wanted to undress her. Within seconds Jake took her t-shirt and bra off. Cathryn laid back down and watched him. He had both of her boots off in another few seconds. He caressed her legs, her waist, then unbuckled her belt. Undid the button on her jeans then pulled down the zipper. He grabbed a handful of jeans and panties. She raised her hips as he slid them down her body. Jake stood back and stared at her with that unbelievable smile of his. She watched his eyes roam from her eyes to her breasts, at which time he licked his lips. Her body heated from the look of longing in his eyes. She felt beautiful, sexy and desired. The pool in between her legs increased as his eyes roamed further down her body, his nostrils flaring as he inhaled. His eyes moved back up to hers, they turned the deepest green. She smiled as he stood there looking at her with that magnificent smile of his.

"What's with that smile?"

"Just admiring the most beautiful work of art I've ever seen. The goddess was having an awesome day the day you were born."

Slowly Cathryn raised the hem of his sweater with her foot. "Am I supposed to be naked alone?"

Jake toed off his boots, reached over the back of his head to pull off his sweater then threw it across the room. His pants followed right after that. When he stood her eyes slowly moved from his intense eyes to his perfect nose, down to his chiseled chin. The dusting of five o'clock shadow gave him a distinctive ruggedly handsome look. The dimples in his cheeks when he smiled were breathtaking.

His body was covered with nice, beautiful hair that outlined every muscle and striation. He had a six-pack that Cathryn wanted to lick over and over again. She trailed the line of hair down to his cock. Her eyes grew wide.

"Holy shit!" burst from her lips.

He was beautifully built and sported a cock that would make a stallion develop low self-esteem.

"They make condoms big enough for that thing?"

Jake chuckled then crawled slowly onto the bed and over her. She marveled the way his muscles rippled as he moved. His scent continued to overpower her senses as her pussy creamed with anticipation. She caressed his chest and arms; she treasured how he felt under her hands. She realized at that moment she liked hairy men, and this hairy one in particular.

Cathryn was lost in a euphoric haze as his hands roamed from one end of her body to the other. The heat from his hands as he caressed her legs felt terrific and increased to magnificent as his hands slid down to her toes then back up her legs. His hands roamed around her butt, then her waist to her breasts. She arched her back when he massaged, then rubbed her nipples between his thumb and forefinger. She moaned and placed her hands on his, and he tweaked her now stiff nubs.

He took her mouth in a forceful, passionate kiss that took her breath as he never stopped his concentration on her breasts. He trailed kisses down her chin; he paused for a moment and nuzzled that section where her neck and shoulder met. He nibbled then continued a trail of tiny kisses down to her full round mounds. He had great hands, a little callused from working around the house, but his touch was soft. He touched her as if he cherished her body like a goddess she now felt like.

***

'I knew it.'

Jake knew her breasts were a perfect fit for his big hands. He loved how he could palm the sides. Jake lowered his head to the left one then took her nipple into his mouth and sucked hard all the while he rolled her other nipple to a peak with his thumb and forefinger. He knew he must be doing something right as she arched her back, urging him on.

He felt the vise grip of her nails as she moaned and dug into his shoulders and hair. He took the other one into his mouth and sucked harder, flicked the dark chocolate chip with his tongue, then moved it back and forth. He made sure one was just as excited to be touched as the other. She wrapped her legs around his waist, arched more in response to his touch and kisses. Her response let him know how much she loved everything he did to her and not to stop.

Jake reluctantly broke his attention on her breasts and moved down, planting a trail of kisses down her body. Her skin felt like silk, warmed to his touch. Goosebumps formed as he lightly blew warm air, teasing her while he progressed downward. His hands smoothed over her waist then her hips, he continued to lick and taste the salty perspiration that formed on her skin. When he reached her navel, he put his lips together and blew. She pleased him with a giggle.

Slowly Jake continued down toward his destination, as he ran his fingers over her silky skin. He finally reached his primary purpose. His ultimate universal focus, her pussy. Jake spread her legs wide with his shoulders. He stopped there on his stomach and gazed up into her eyes. What he saw almost undid him. The desire in her eyes was beautiful, the deep amber color so intense. The whole time he stared into her eyes he lightly, teasingly rubbed her clit. He needed to see how she would respond to his touch.

He watched her breathing increase, perspiration beaded on her skin. She started to roll her hips into the rhythm of his teasing. He broke his concentration from her eyes to focus on her beautiful pussy before him. He parted her folds to her holiest of holies. The color of her was a beautiful deep purple. Her clit engorged the more he teased her. It called to him, waiting to be sucked, licked. Her nectar seeped out as an invitation to taste. Jake knew he drove her crazy with his teasing.

"Ahh…Jake…baby, you're killing me here. Jake…baby…please."

That was all he needed to hear, he couldn't let his lady wait any longer. His thumb slowly massaged her clit up and down. He slowly inserted one finger as he continued to attend to her clit. She gasped as he moved his finger in then out very slowly. Her walls constricted, trying to pull him in further. Gradually he added another finger as he licked and sucked her beautiful button. Her walls pulsated faster as he finger-fucked her. Her moans kept in rhythm with the motions of his hands. He held her hips down with his other hand as he pumped in and out while his tongue continued his assault on her clit.

"Oh, yes! Just like that!"

***

Cathryn felt as if she floated on air. She curled her hands into his hair as she tried to anchor herself. Cathryn tried to keep her hips still but what he did to her clit was marvelous. Lost in her own sensations, she couldn't think, all she could do was feel. Cathryn felt the friction of his big fingers sliding in and out. Lost in her sensations she felt far away, she heard moans but couldn't believe they generated from her. She held tight to his hair to keep his face right where she needed him. Cathryn felt her orgasm build, it moved over her body in waves that amplified in intensity. With every thrust of his fingers and flick of his tongue, a surge of energy rolled over her as she called his name. Before Cathryn was aware, out of nowhere her orgasm slammed into her like a wrecking ball. She screamed his name as her being shattered.

Cathryn barely caught her breath as her brain returned to somewhat functional mode. Jake continued his rhythm of his fingers as she rode out her orgasm. She felt light-headed, her vision a little blurred, but she felt terrific. No man had ever given her such a fantastic orgasm ever in her life. A little dazed, she raised her head as Jake stared at her with that grin. His lower face looked like a glazed donut. She smiled back, held her arms to him as Jake crawled up to her. He kissed her, hot, heavy and ravenous, and she tasted herself on his lips.

***

'I knew she would taste as good as she looked.'

He couldn't get enough. Cathryn's lips were made for kissing. Jake quickly moved to his nightstand to grab a condom. He ripped it open with such ferocity, a growl escaped his throat.

Cathryn raised her eyebrows in astonishment. He was beyond ready to take her, serve her and brand her as his.

Once sheathed, he leaned over her, looked directly into her eyes. He liked the way she touched him. Her hands caressed his chest and shoulders. She felt him as if she worshiped his body. He took both of her hands into his, raised them above her head. He placed both of hers into one of his. He grabbed his cock and positioned it at her entrance.

She gasped, "Damn, I can't believe this!"

"What?"

"This. This is happening. This isn't just a dream."

Jake grinned, and then slowly pushed into her, inch by agonizing inch. He wanted, no he needed to feel her walls constrict around his cock. And they did. She was deliciously wet and tight. He slowly inched his way out then crept his way in again. He gave her body a chance to adjust to his size each time his slid into her. With each thrust, she gasped, moaned and curled and uncurled her hands, trying to grasp the air. She wrapped her legs around his waist. She pressed her heels into his backside to match his thrusts.

"Jake… deeper… I want all of it" she pleaded between moans.

He obliged his lady then buried himself to the hilt. Jake couldn't believe this was happening. This wasn't a dream. This was better than his dream. Live Cathryn was so much better than dream Cathryn. Her kisses were more intense. Her skin was smoother than he could ever have imagined. She called his name with each thrust. Oh, Goddess, this was a dream come true. Slowly, steadily, his thrusts gained intensity.

The harder he pushed, the more her pussy tightened around his cock, and the more he grunted. He pressed her body into the mattress to mark her as his territory. He dropped his face to her neck as he thrust harder then released a long deep growl.

She screamed, tightening her hands on his.

"Oh, goddess, yes, Jake! Yes...yes...yes!"

Jake felt his orgasm surge forward. He threw his head back with a growl. Jake released himself then collapsed on top of her. He groaned and took deep breaths as he rode out the rest of his orgasm. He planted kisses on her cheeks, her ear, then stopped to nibble on her earlobe and down her neck. Gently he bit then sucked her neck. She moaned and turned her head to give him better access. He licked her neck up to her chin as she let out another slow, erotic moan which made him hard all over again.

He slowly pulled out from her as she released a small whimper of protest. He planted a kiss on her cheek, got up, threw the condom in his wastebasket by his nightstand and went into his bathroom.

***

Cathryn lay in his bed, her eyes closed, and smiled. She had never felt more sexually satisfied ever before in her entire adult life. Cathryn heard water running in her comfortable daze. Then a moment later the bed dipped, and she felt warmth between her legs. She raised her head and gave Jake a strange look. He cleaned her with a warm washcloth. She started to protest, but her instincts told her to let him pamper her. She'd never had a man clean her after sex before. She could get used to this. No man had ever spoiled her, not even what's-his-name. She couldn't remember that fucktard's name if her life depended on it. The memory of him faded as quickly as it surfaced.

Hot, sweaty hair plastered to her head, she let out a slow exhale. Cathryn felt calm, serene. She let out another slow exhale and moaned. When Jake finished cleaning her, he took the washcloth back to his bathroom then came back to lie on top of her. She spread her legs to make room for him. She enjoyed the feel of his weight on her. He balanced his weight on his elbows.

She loved the way he felt against her. He fit perfectly, as if he belonged there.

He planted small kisses on her lips and nose.

"Are you hungry? I think we worked up a little bit of an appetite. And I'm sure there are some questions we should ask each other. Like last names and other important things."

"Actually, I am hungry."

Chapter 9

Cathryn stood in the doorway that separated Jake's kitchen and the great room. She wore one of his dress shirts that fell just above her knees. For a man with thick muscles, she was amazed how smooth he moved around his kitchen. He stood at the butcher block in the center, preparing venison steaks. She knew that scent of meat.

'He must cook a lot.'

Jake's back was to her. Her attention brought back to him, she licked her lips as she watched his back muscles ripple as he moved around the butcher block. His jeans rode low on his hips. She marveled at his magnificent ass, oh my goddess, that ass just begged to be nibbled on.

She momentarily broke her concentration from Jake's ass to notice the design of his kitchen. Dark wood cabinets, huge six-burner gas stove with grill, black appliances, and granite countertops complemented the entire design.

He turned around toward the grill to put the steaks on. He looked up, saw Cathryn, then smiled.

'That smile should be illegal.'

He pointed to the kitchen table to the right for her to have a seat. That way she could be close to talk to and not be in his way as he worked.

As they talked, she found out how much they had in common. They both spent time in the military. Their families had been in Las Vegas since before the building of the Hoover Dam. She discovered their spiritual beliefs were somewhat the same, the same mental disciplines with small differences in training. Daily meditations were mandatory to control their spirit animals as well as themselves. Cathryn talked about her first shift. Her Nana told her it was time after the start of her first cycle. Her change into her wolf was easy and fun. She felt energized, she jumped around like the junior pup she was. Her Nana let her run and play.

She enjoyed her first run with her Nana. But when they returned home, the shift back was not as easy as she thought it would be. It wasn't easy for her to visualize her human self. It took about an hour, but she eventually focused her magick on shifting back. The whole time her grandmother laughed at her. Because Cathryn's father had the same issue. The more she talked about her life, the more she felt relaxed around Jake.

While the steaks grilled, he started the vegetables. He cut them with swift precision. He placed them in a cast iron pan, added seasonings which filled the kitchen with their delicious aroma.

'If the man cooks as well as he fucks, I'm in serious trouble.'

***

She looked delicious wearing his shirt.

'I may never wash that shirt again.'

Jake loved listening to her talk. He let her lead most of the conversation because she fascinated him. As they continued to share their backgrounds, he told her some of his military experiences. Not too much because a lot of his missions were classified. He sensed her relax with him.

He finally shared that he was part owner of the casino. A wave of intense emotion hit him. He looked up at her and saw a frown on Cathryn's face that worried him.

"What's wrong? Did I say something wrong?"

"No, nothing's wrong."

He felt she tried to convince herself more than him. Jake crossed the kitchen to her, squatted down, and took her hands.

"What's the problem, baby? I know there's something's wrong. I can feel it, please tell me."

Cathryn kept her eyes on the floor.

"So, it this some fling for you? You obviously knew who I was. I work for you, after all."

Jake kneeled down on both knees. He cupped her cheek with his right hand. He raised her head to look into her beautiful amber eyes.

"No, Cat. I didn't know who you were when I met you at the lounge last night. Except for your name on your badge. I went to my uncle, who's the other owner, and asked if knew anything about you. The only information he gave me was how long you worked there and information about your family, that's all. I wanted to hear all the essential things from your lips."

He gazed deep into her eyes.

"Baby, trust me. What we did tonight was not just a one-night thing. At least not for me. What we did tonight was beautiful, intense, and damn near mind-blowing. Even better than my dream I had last night."

Cathryn raised her eyes to look at him then.

"I had a dream about you last night, too."

Jake's eyebrows shot up. He stood, pulled her with him at the same time. Wrapped his arms around her waist, pulled her close then kissed her. She leaned into him and his kiss. He slowly released their kiss.

"We better stop this before the food burns. Besides, I'm curious to hear about your dream."

He swatted her on her butt and went back to cooking.

"Oh, by the way. You're the first woman I have ever cooked for."

***

Cathryn like him, a lot. He was literally the man of her dreams. And now she found out he was her boss, which spelled trouble. The whole time he spoke, she looked at his lips; he had very sexy lips. But then he mentioned his dream. She looked into his eyes. She remembered her dream and how vivid it was. Then her Nana's words came back to her; *'Trust him.'*

Cathryn swore she was about to have another orgasm. She moaned as she smelled the steak he prepared. Damn, but this man could cook. She put the last piece of steak in her mouth, tilted her head back. She chewed, swallowed, then moaned again.

When she lowered her head, she looked at Jake. He had a look of pure satisfaction and desire. He stood, adjusted his jeans, and cleared the dishes. Poor thing looked like he had a difficult time walking. He did sport a considerable bulge when he turned back toward her.

He held his hand to her, helped her from the chair. His hand slid down to her hip. He pulled her close to his side as they walked into the great room. She wrapped her arm around his waist as he led her toward the couch. She saw the discarded bottle of wine and the wine glasses from earlier. She'd wondered what had happened to them. He opened the bottle as she sat in the corner of the couch and stretched her legs across it. He lifted her legs, sat close to let her legs drape over his lap. He poured them both glasses.

"Now, baby. Tell me about your dream."

"You go first."

She felt the warmth spread throughout her body as he began to tell her his dream. She wasn't sure if it was the wine, his erotic story, or how softly he stroked her legs. Wetness began to pool between her legs again as he finished. She watched Jake inhale deep as he kissed her with a smile on his lips. Heat rushed through her, which made her cheeks warm.

"Now, baby, tell me yours."

She was already warm when she started her story. About a quarter of the way through, her body began to heat up even more. Her skin felt hot under his hands. She became entranced by her story as she explained in detail how she felt when he was on top of her and the things he did to her in her dream. She felt his cock stiffen under her leg the more she told her story. It damn near stood straight up when she adjusted herself to get comfortable. She looked into his eyes when she finished her story. His breathing seemed to increase when she was entirely done.

"Damn, baby. I like your dream better."

Jake took her wine glass, set both on the coffee table. He held her face then kissed her. Cathryn moved her hand up his arm to his shoulder, up to his hair. She wove her fingers through his waves to his scalp. His hair was soft. She loved how the waves curled around her fingers. A burst of his arousal scent increased the wetness between her legs. His kiss became more passionate when she curled her hand into a fist in his hair.

His hand trailed down her body to her hips and legs. He caressed back up her body under his shirt to her breasts. His hand cupped her breast as she moaned when he rubbed then rolled her nipple to full nub.

Slowly he trailed his hand back down her body toward 'Happy Valley.' Cathryn opened her legs to invite him in. He slid one finger past her folds. Slowly Jake massaged her clit with his thumb. Her moans mingled with his as he pushed another finger into her. She began panting, begging him to take her now. Jake trailed kisses down her neck, then up to her ear and nuzzled her neck. He released a growl as he slid his fingers in and out. The vibrations flicked at her nerve endings through her body as she released a long, erotic moan then creamed all over his hand. Jake took her lips hard and passionately. Removed his fingers from her, licked his fingers, then moaned.

"Delicious."

He cradled her in his arms, carried her back to his bedroom. She hoped he planned to make love to her all night. With their shifting sexual appetite, he could accomplish that.

Chapter 10

Jake gazed at the beautiful woman who lay beside him. Fascinated by how the sunlight touched her skin. The light accented her high cheekbones, her black lashes fanned out against her cheeks. Her full, juicy, pouty lips glistened in the morning light. He wanted to kiss them every chance he could.

He felt bliss as he woke up next to her, something he'd never felt before; it felt right. He never wanted this feeling to change. What this was or where this would go, he didn't know. But he refused to let anyone, or anything take her away from him. His wolf was in complete agreement.

Cathryn moaned, stretched. She bumped her hand against his forehead as she yawned.

"What time is it?"

"5:30…am."

Her eyes flew open wide.

"Oh shit! Oh, I have to go. My roommate is probably having a cow or a deer with a full rack of antlers about now."

"No problem. I have to help my uncle with some things at his house today." Jake leaned in and kissed her.

"I wish I didn't have to go. I would rather keep you in my bed for the rest of your weekend." He trailed kisses to her earlobe and nibbled.

"Mmmmm, Goddess, I would love that, too. But my best friend Patty is probably freaking out by now. And I think I left my cell home."

Her words trailed off. She moaned as Jake nuzzled her neck.

"I don't have any extra clothes here. Everything else I need is at home."

"You wouldn't need clothes if you're in my bed all weekend." He captured her lips again in a deep passionate kiss.

Jake decided they should drive back to her cabin. Shifting during the day was very dangerous with hunters out. It always caused people to freak when they saw more than one wolf running through the woods close to their cabins. Sometimes, it made a good laugh. But it caused too many problems.

He helped Cathryn climb into his truck. He buckled her seatbelt for her. She gave him a strange look.

"You know I can do this by myself."

"I know. But this gives me another reason to get close to kiss you."

He couldn't get enough of her lips. They were addicting, she was addicting. Jake walked around the front of his truck then climbed into the driver's seat. He enjoyed the Cheshire cat grin spread across his face.

She told him about a back road to her house. Once they were on the way, she leaned her head on his shoulder then drifted off to sleep again with her hand on his lap. He kissed the top of her head, which caused her to purr and snuggle closer to him. He nudged her when they reached the turnoff to her house.

As he turned into her driveway, four dogs ran toward the gate. The dogs stopped and stared at him when they climbed out of his truck. Cathryn stepped through the gate first as her dogs greeted her. There were one female and three males. The female walked toward Cathryn as she bent down to pet her. Jake never hesitated as he followed her. Her dogs were beautiful.

'Malamutes.'

Perfect for a wolf shifter. He felt their hesitation and curiosity. He watched the other three, and they watched him.

"It's okay. Come here."

Cathryn patted her thighs. They took their time as they walked toward her but never took their eyes off of Jake. The female finally relented and walked toward Jake first, sniffed him. He bent down, petted her head. Let her smell the palms of his hands. She rose on her hind legs then licked his face. The males stood by Cathryn until Jake stepped further away from her to the left. All three walked toward him and stood still. He let them sniff him, then he squatted down to their level. He opened his hands, palms up. One by one they sniffed his palms.

"That's strange. Usually they don't act this way with people. Jake, what are you doing?"

Jake didn't answer her at first. He touched each. Their earlier hesitation faded away. Each one rose up and licked his face. Then all four walked to the other side of the large yard.

"The boys and I needed to talk. Man, to man, wolf to dog, so to speak."

"What did you say to them?"

"Just men talk, dear. Nothing to concern yourself with, woman..." He swatted her butt and grinned.

As they walked through the door, a woman with light brown curly hair stood at the bottom of the stairs with her arms crossed under her breasts.

"You know, it's about damn time you decided to come home. Just because I may know that you're okay doesn't mean you can't call me to let me know you're ...okay."

The woman stopped her rant when she realized he followed Cathryn into the house. Cathryn apologized then introduced her roommate Patty to him. The expression on Patty's face as she shook Jake's hand was a look of wow then relief. Patty smiled then excused herself.

Cathryn turned and bumped right into Jake. He caught her, wrapped her in his arms as close as possible. She wrapped her arms around his waist and slid her hands up his back. Jake took her lips with his for a full, possessive kiss. His senses tingled, the sensations he felt became intense. Jake couldn't tell if the feelings were his or hers. But he knew this felt right.

He reluctantly broke their kiss.

"I have to go. I'm going to miss you a lot," he whispered against her lips between kisses.

He made sure he held onto her butt, pulled her close, and rocked his hips side to side. Just to let her know how much he would miss her.

"I'm going to miss you, too." A frown formed on her face.

"What's wrong, baby?"

"This is happening too fast for me. I'm not used to feeling like this so soon after meeting someone. It's so…It's so intense."

"I know. I feel the same way, but it also feels right."

He leaned down for another hungry kiss.

Slowly they broke the kiss. Jake kissed her on her nose, pulled out his cell. He texted her his number. With one more kiss, he said, "I'll call you later."

"Okay."

***

Cathryn walked toward the couch pit, plopped down onto the cushions. Moaned then stretched. She felt relaxed, content, and knew she sported a look of bliss with a shit-eating grin.

Patty walked in from the kitchen.

"So…you finally got laid?"

Cathryn looked up at her.

"Madam, I will have you know I did not just get laid. I was properly fucked, and well I might say!"

Cathryn received applause and a whistle from her best friend.

"It's about damn time. Now spill, how many orgasms did he give you?"

Cathryn closed her eyes, moaned again.

"I don't know. I lost track after the first two…in a row."

Patty gave her another round of applause then asked for details. Cathryn obliged. She told her about the run, to the bed. Several times in the bed and the couch, then the shower.

"He's just as good in the kitchen, as he is in bed."

"The most important part, Patty, the man cleans up after himself every time. And I'm not talking about wiping down the counters either."

As Cathryn told her best friend about her night and morning, her panties became wet again. She took a deep breath to settle her emotions. Cathryn finished her story of him being half-owner of the Preserve. She didn't know how it would affect their future relationship. Or how it would impact her job.

She thought as far as her job. It would go one of two ways. Roger would start to harass her by assigning her the crappy areas to work. Or kiss her ass and award her the best areas to work. Then there were her co-workers, especially the catty ones. They would either start to talk about her behind her back or would not speak to her at all. With so much on her mind, she decided to go to bed. She was tired; since Jake said he couldn't sleep, she couldn't sleep.

"Oh, before you hit the sack. You left your cell home. You have some missed calls. Wanna guess from whom? One good guess, you won't believe who the calls are from."

Cathryn raised her head, then gave her best friend a strange look.

"Who?"

Patty handed her, her cell. Cathryn looked at the missed calls ID. She sat straight up on the couch.

"Fucking son of a bitch!"

She forgot to block his number.

"Yep, right on the head."

Chapter 11

Malcolm Sawyer, a former Marine Scout Sniper. Who graduated 1st in his class in sniper school loved his job and did it well. Sometimes, too well. He served one tour in Afghanistan and received a dishonorable discharge for dereliction of duty. He took out a target to soon, which screwed up a mission that nearly cost a team of Marines their lives.

Growing up in Henderson, Nevada his family had connections to some of the good old boys from Vegas' founding fathers. So, when he decided to purchase the Hard Target Gun Range, that little spot on his separation papers didn't hurt his chances to acquire it. The Henderson County Sheriff was an old friend of his family but was forced to ignore that part of his background check.

Malcolm's father always fed on his insecurities, especially with the girls he met in high school. As he became older, his father competed with him for women. His father told him he was nothing if he couldn't keep a woman. Ironically Malcolm's mother left the family when he was young. According to his father, he was too much man for her to handle anyway.

Malcolm was not happy when Cathryn dumped him. He was pissed. How dare she throw him aside as if he was nothing? He knew what was best for her. He was in control of her and all she did.

She was like the rest of those weak, sexually-repressed bitches. Their lives were his to control. It wasn't his fault she couldn't be sexually satisfied. He was good at what he did. Like the rest of those frigid bitches, he worked hard to give her an orgasm. If she didn't achieve one that was her fault; his satisfaction was more important. He'd make sure she paid for leaving him. He discarded women when he was through with them.

He decided to use his connections and some of his not so lovely friends to get the latest information on her.

***

Cathryn had been on Jake's mind all day. After he left her house, he went back home to shower again to rub himself. He had to try to get her out of his system before he arrived at his uncle's. It worked for a little while, at least. He thought of last night's and this morning's lovemaking, which aroused him again by the time he arrived at his uncle's house. Hopefully, all the physical work would curb his insatiable appetite for her.

He kept his mind off her for a short time as he poured cement and laid bricks for his uncle's new project. The finished bar-b-que pit was big enough to roast a side of a cow. There she was again, on his mind. Jake felt she thought of him, too. Not that he picked up her actual thoughts, but he felt her emotions and hoped they were for him.

***

Jonathan had a ball harassing his nephew. Several times, he caught Jake daydreaming. In the middle of a conversation, Jake's eyes drifted off somewhere. Jonathan called his name several times. When Jake finally acknowledged him, Jonathan asked him what was so important on his mind. Although he knew what was so important or who was so important. Jake looked at his uncle, smiled with a surprised look.

Jonathan was happy his nephew was in a good mood and finally relaxed. He worried he'd never let himself find a good woman. From the emotions Jonathan felt from Jake, this Cathryn seemed like a good woman. But he needed to check things out for himself. What better way to get to know her than by breaking in the new bar-b-que pit with a party. Meet her face to face; that would give him a chance to get a sniff to see what her real intentions are.

Chapter 12

Cathryn floated on air as she drove to work. Her body still tingled from all of Jake's attention. The rest of her weekend wasn't too eventful. She played with the dogs, hung out with Patty. Sometimes in the middle of their conversations her mind drifted to Jake. She pictured the things he did to her body; her response kept her in a constant state of arousal.

Sometimes Malcolm also made an appearance in her mind. She wondered what he wanted after all this time. She hadn't heard from him in almost a year. Now, of all times for him to make an appearance. She'd be ready for him and any of his mind games he loved to play.

Her workday started off bizarrely when she when she arrived at the casino. An uneasy feeling washed over her as soon as she crossed the threshold. Her instincts kicked into high gear. As she changed into her uniform, some of the usual cocktail waitresses spoke to her. But then a few who'd never talked to her before said hello. The latter always acted as if they were too good to acknowledge her.

After she signed in at the office, she started to go to her assigned area when Roger stopped her. He asked her if she wouldn't mind working the lounge again for the rest of the week. The waitress who usually covered it put in her notice to quit. Then she walked out that same day.

"No problem."

She was a bit surprised by Roger. This was the first time he'd actually spoken to her as if she were an actual person, rather than someone beneath him. It began as she'd predicted.

'The ass kissing has now commenced!'

She said hello to Nick when she arrived at the lounge bar. He told her he remembered where he recognized the big guy from the other day. He showed her the magazine about the local casino businesses. Jake and another man appeared on the front cover. Nick flipped through it to an article that featured Jake and the other gentleman. Nick told her the article was about Jake becoming part owner. There were other pictures inside that showed the same man and Jake again. The date on the magazine was six years ago. One picture caught her attention: Jake, with some woman on his arm at a party in one of the casino's ballrooms. Jake looked a lot younger, and the picture looked like they were at his high school prom. Questions raced through her mind.

'Who is this woman? Is she still in his life?'

***

Malcolm sat at the back of the lounge and realized how much he wanted Cathryn back. Not because he loved her, no fucking way. She needed to be taught a lesson or two. His blood raced straight to his cock as he watched her approach the station. He would have her again, and this time he'd teach her who was in command.

She'd do whatever he said, no matter what. No matter how long it took, he would have her again. Once he finished with her, she'd disappear for good. He smiled at the thought of all the holes in the desert that could be filled. She did look good, sexier than he remembered, for now. He only stayed away because of how she dumped him. But now was his time, then she would pay.

He had to be subtle, take his time to get back into her good graces. She needed to trust him again. He'd have to get her away from that bitch roommate of hers. Oh, and those dogs. How he hated those fucking dogs. She'd be his again once they were all out of his way.

***

That strange sensation Cathryn felt when she walked into the casino increased as she walked back to the lounge bar.

Something was wrong. She felt nauseous. Bile rose in her throat. The hairs on the back of her neck stood on end. She looked around the lounge, then toward the back. She saw him. Malcolm…that son of a bitch was here, at her job. He stared at her with a strange look on his face that she didn't like. Her wolf jumped up on all fours, ready and eager for a fight.

She grabbed her tray to continue her rounds through the lounge. She pasted a fake smile on her face as she moved from table to table, taking drink orders. Slowly she approached Malcolm, dropped her smile, then glared at him, but politely said, "Hi."

"Hello."

"What are you doing here?"

"Ordering a drink. Is that a problem?"

He responded without a smile. He looked her up and down, then a small smile crossed his face.

"And waiting for a friend."

"Right. What will you have to drink?" Cathryn tried her damndest to remain calm. It would not go over well if she tried to hurt him or tell him to get the fuck out. Even from those trying to kiss her ass.

"The usual. You do remember what I like. Right?"

"No, Malcolm. I don't. It's been a while. Why don't you remind me?"

Her patience began to wear thin.

The air around her became thick with tension. She needed to get away from Malcolm, now. She needed to clear her head to figure out what and why he decided to make an appearance at her job. Of all the casinos in Las Vegas and Henderson, he'd appeared here. Now.

Malcolm dropped his jaw then palmed his chest. He pretended his feelings were hurt.

"Oh, Cat, that hurts. You honestly don't remember? I'll have a Jack, straight up. Remember it next time."

Cathryn raised her eyebrows, took a step toward him and clenched her fist so tight she cracked her pen. She glared at him for five seconds, then turned and walked toward the bar.

Pissed off didn't come close to how she felt now. She slammed her tray onto the bar, placed her orders with Nick, then took deep breaths in and out. She drummed her nails on the bar as she continued her deep, cleansing breaths to force herself to calm down. She needed to remain in control and calm. Nick gave her a worried look.

"Are you okay?"

Nick looked over his shoulder at Malcolm because Cathryn glared in that direction.

She took another deep breath, shrugged her shoulders.

"Yes, I'm fine."

After several more cleansing breaths, Cathryn finally calmed herself. But her wolf wouldn't calm down. It pushed itself close to the surface, ready to pounce if Malcolm did anything stupid. She put her drink orders on her tray then brought them to her guests. The closer she approached Malcolm the worse the nauseous feeling became. His scent was dark and dangerous, nothing like before. He must still be pissed she dumped him. Not her problem; it's time he moved on.

After leaving all those messages, he showed up here. If that's not bad enough, Jake...Jake! Oh, good goddess! Oh shit!

That's one problem she didn't need now. If Malcolm did anything stupid, Jake would tear him apart then hide all the body parts in the desert. She'd heard some of Malcolm's military stories. She realized the only reason he told her some of his harrowing past was to prove how much of a badass he was and tried to intimidate her. But Malcolm wasn't a shifter. If Jake's wolf's instincts sensed danger to himself or her, there was no way of knowing what Jake's wolf would do to Malcolm.

***

Jake tracked Cathryn's scent through the casino, which has been burned into his memory. He carried two dozen red roses in a lead-crystal vase. A red ribbon tied around it. But another scent stopped him dead in his tracks. A smell he didn't like.

He stopped in between two rows of slot machines a few rows away from the lounge bar. A man sat in the back of the lounge, staring at his woman with malice in his eyes. Jake's wolf jumped up, ready to attack and defend their mate. Jake had seen that look too many times. He'd worn that look a few times himself.

'His woman.' That felt strange, but he welcomed it.

Who the fuck was this man and what did he want with Cat? Jake watched her make two more rounds through the lounge. Jake focused his hearing. He dropped the background noise around him. He tried to listen to their conversation. She wasn't happy to see this man. Whoever this asshole was, he needed to know whose territory he was trying to piss in. Uncontrollable rage washed over him, fast and hard. It came from Cathryn. She seemed to know this guy and didn't like him one bit. Jake decided it was time to make his move.

Jake prowled toward the lounge. He tried to sneak up while her back was to him. She quickly turned around with her hands on her hips and a big beautiful smile.

"You seriously thought you could sneak up on me?"

When she saw the roses, she threw her arms around his neck, pulled his head down for a kiss. Jake wrapped his free arm around her waist, pulled her tight against him and responded to her kiss. Jake broke their kiss, lifted his eyes to see the strange man glare at them. The stranger's scent became more intense and dangerous.

He handed her the vase; she closed her eyes as she smelled the roses. When she turned toward the bar, Jake wrapped her in another embrace, nuzzled her neck while he glared at the stranger.

Cathryn handed the vase to the bartender, who put the roses behind the bar on the shelf. She tried to turn around, but Jake had her pinned tight to his body to nuzzle her more.

"Jake, stop that. I have to get back to work!"

"I'm establishing my male dominance. To let all the other males know you're mine. This casino is mine. The surrounding territory is mine!" he whispered in her ear. "Don't look up. Who is that man at the back of the lounge staring at you?"

He felt her tense as she inhaled then exhaled but kept her head still.

"An ex-boyfriend. I'll tell you about him later."

Jake lifted his hand to her chin, turned her head toward him.

"Okay." He kissed her cheek. "I'm going back up to my office. Have dinner with me when you get off work?"

"That sounds great."

***

'Who's the new guy? He must be the one she left me for.'

Questions formed in Malcolm's mind on his drive home. It didn't matter; he'd remove him, too. Then Cathryn would know her place. He told Cathryn he waited for an old friend, which wasn't a complete lie. She was the former friend, but she didn't need to know that. Not yet. He needed to get the lay of the land again. He had to find out what she'd been up to for the last year. It seemed this new guy was it. Malcolm would put out his feelers to get as much information on them both and anyone else connected with her. He'd start with that bartender who kept eyeing him. He and Cat seemed close.

Chapter 13

Jake listened to Cathryn as she told him about her work night as they ate a late dinner in the café. She told him about some of the male patrons who flirted with her. Jake felt a bit of jealous rage from his wolf. He took a couple of deep breaths then tempered it down. This was her job, and she couldn't help but look so damn sexy in her uniform. He'd have to thank and curse his uncle on the design. They were designed almost like Playboy Bunny uniforms. Instead of cottontails, they wore wolf tails. He remembered when he first saw her in it the other day. He gained a raging hard-on and kept a continuous one ever since. He'd already made plans to go home with her, take her all night and well into the morning. Especially now since her ex had decided to make an appearance.

After a long conversation about each other's night, she finally told him about her relationship with Malcolm. How long they were together and why she broke it off. Malcolm didn't accept the breakup, in the beginning. He couldn't believe she dumped him. Malcolm accused her of cheating on him. She was asked several times if there another man because that was the only reason she would leave him.

Jake felt she didn't tell him the whole story, like she held back something very import from him. This had his wolf pacing back and forth. But he decided not to push this just yet. But eventually he would get her to open up more. But after this conversation, he made a definite decision to follow Cathryn home tonight. He had a bad feeling about her ex and didn't like the look or smell of that asshole. He wasn't taking any chances with this Malcolm. He might try to get back into her life or, worse, try to hurt her.

As he turned his truck into the driveway, he pulled up behind Cathryn's SUV. He noticed the dogs stood near the west fence. They looked tense, as if they were ready to attack something or someone. He stepped out of his truck and felt something wrong. The dogs ran toward them, happy to see them. He looked around and sniffed, but not to be noticeable. He didn't want to alarm Cathryn. He caught a scent of something familiar but very, very faint. So, faint he had a hard time separating it from the foliage of the mountains. There was something there that he didn't like. The scent was sour and oily. Whoever or whatever it was, one thing was for sure: He was not leaving this house tonight.

***

Cathryn had been aroused and wet all night. Her instincts had sharpened since she'd been with Jake. Her senses had also honed to the point Cathryn could feel when Jake crossed the threshold of the casino. She'd received roses before, but never two dozen in a beautiful lead- crystal vase. That was just fantastic.

Patty's SUV wasn't there when they arrived. She must be on another date in town or at the Mt. Charleston ski lodge. They went there sometimes just to get out of the house. When Cathryn pulled up to the fence, she noticed the dogs stood at the edge of the west fence. They faced the mountain and didn't move until she and Jake stepped out of their vehicles.

She remembered them acting that way toward Malcolm all the time. Worse, they didn't like him at all. They never went anywhere near him. But whenever he was around they would always be around her, blocking him from getting too close to her. At that time, they showed they had better taste and sense of smell than she had. They ran toward her and Jake as they walked through the gate.

Cathryn walked in front of Jake when a scent hit her. She raised her face slowly and inhaled. Cathryn knew that smell. It was faint, but she knew without a doubt who that sour, oily stench belonged to.

The cabin was cold as they entered. The embers in the fireplace were almost ash. After she put her coat on the rack by the door, Cathryn headed toward the kitchen to get the dogs their food.

Still pissed, her mind focused on Malcolm and why he was at the casino tonight. The same thought ran through her mind all night.

'Was he really waiting for a friend, or was he there to start shit with me?'

Cathryn left out specific details from Jake. But now was not the time, no need to involve him more. Not just yet. Malcolm was her problem, her chaos. She'd take care of him herself. She did it once before, but he apparently didn't get the point.

She thought back to their short relationship. Malcolm tried to control her every move. Almost from the very beginning. He told her how to dress for their dates, how to wear her hair so it wasn't too flattering. He wanted her to stop wearing makeup. He told her she didn't need any. He accused her of flirting with the male patrons, and that was the reason she wore so much makeup all the time. On numerous occasions, he told her she needed to lose some weight. Cathryn knew she was curvy; she worked out all the time, long before she met him. Then he started continually hanging out around the casino, in her assigned sections to keep an eye on her.

After a while, she had had enough. She told Malcolm to back off. He did for a while. He pretended to be okay with everything. But then he turned back to his old self in a hurry. He wouldn't give her room to breathe. He tried to pressure her into quitting her job. He said he had more than enough money to support them both. But when she refused he got physical, and she put him in his place. That was one control freak she had to get rid of. From that point on, no man would ever control her ever again.

Jake's tension increased as he walked into her house. He looked around to make sure no one was there who didn't belong. His Force Recon Marine training taught him to always be aware of his surroundings. Memorize every detail no matter how small. He had a feeling of dread since her ex showed at the casino, and he still couldn't shake it. He took in the scent of the house. The only scents he picked up were Cat's, Patty's, and the dogs, which was a good thing. That meant the asshole never stepped foot in her house, at least not tonight.

He followed her into the kitchen then glanced around. The design and function impressed him. He liked the natural flow of it all. Stainless steel appliances throughout, and a table with four chairs sat in the center. Dark cherry wood cabinets with red and black granite countertops. A bay window above the sink that looked out at the expanse of the mountains to the west. That window was big enough to see into. His feeling of dread increased.

Jake watched her every move as she put the vase on the counter then moved toward the dog food bag in the corner. His eyes never left her backside as she bent over the 20lb bag of dog food. As she scooped out the food into four bowls, he thought how much he liked her in that position. He licked his lips as he jeans became a little, no, a lot too tight. Some of his rage eased away but was replaced with a different kind of tension. He walked up behind her as she finished filling the bowls and took them from her.

“Baby, where’s the firewood?”

“Just around the corner, outside to the right.”

Jake took the bowls outside. The dogs sat in front of the door. The scent was gone. Someone had definitely been watching the house and Cathryn. His rage returned. Someone was stupid enough to fuck with his woman.

His wolf pushed itself toward the surface with such force the dogs whined then bowed in submission. He had not felt himself lose control like that in a long time. He’d had his berserker under control for a long, long time now. He took several deep breaths to calm himself and his wolf. He set the bowls down then petted them to calm them and let them know he was in control again.

‘His woman!’

Again, where did that come from? It was too soon to think of her as his woman. Or was it? He was getting used to being around her. His wolf knew she was theirs. No way was anyone going to get anywhere near her to hurt her. He thought if it were this Malcolm person he'd snap his fucking neck.

Jake pulled his senses to the surface. He tasted pine, lavender, sage, and the dogs. The waning moon hung low in the night sky, which gave off just enough light. Not like he needed the light of the moon. He clearly saw up to the top of the tree line.

He started his search at the west fence perimeter for any evidence of the intruder. Then he moved to the left of the cabin. A pool and Jacuzzi were on the side of the cabin. He thought about how much fun they could have in that. He found nothing out of the ordinary. Nothing was disturbed, no prints other than the dogs'.

As he continued around the outside of the cabin, he came upon a small window. A little room at the back of the cabin contained a gym with free weights, a universal machine, and a punching bag.

'Wow, my voluptuous lady is fit, and can take care of herself.'

He moved toward the barn located to the left of the cabin, then proceeded inside. He inhaled but didn't find anyone's scent other than Cathryn and Patty's.

He found the logs stacked right where Cat said they would be. He loaded six logs onto one arm then proceeded back into the house. He was satisfied he didn't find anything disturbed. He stepped on the porch, around the dogs as they lay in a puppy pile by the front door, protecting their mommy.

"What took you so long?"

"I was just looking at things. It's the Recon Marine in me. I needed to make sure all is well out there."

Jake felt guilty for not telling her the whole truth. But the man and his wolf felt the automatic need to protect her from anything and anyone. Especially an ex-boyfriend who gave off a terrible stench.

Cathryn crossed her arms, which pushed her breasts up as she glared at him through squinted eyes. Jake took a deep swallow because he sensed her anger.

***

Cathryn knew what he'd been up to. Jake was just making sure that Malcolm was no longer on or near the property. He was protective, and that was fine. But the fact he hadn't admitted it to her pissed her off.

Jake must think she was weak or that she couldn't take care of herself. Well, he was gravely mistaken. Or maybe he thought she couldn't handle an ex-boyfriend. Which was even more ridiculous. She was a shifter, with the senses and instincts of a wolf. She didn't need a protector. She'd take care of Malcolm Sawyer just as well if not better than the next wolf. And she certainly didn't need another man trying to control her.

Cathryn turned toward the sink to wash her hands as her rage began to build. She didn't know who to be more pissed off with. Malcolm for invading her life again, or Jake for thinking she was weak.

She felt Jake step close behind her. His heat wrapped around her felt great, but she was still pissed. He leaned in close.

"So, what exactly are you so pissed off about?"

She turned her head slightly.

"What makes you think I'm pissed off about anything?"

"Well, you have a tone, you're tense, and I can smell it all over you."

Cathryn grabbed a hand towel, slowly dried her hands, then threw it on the counter. She turned around with her arms folded under her breasts and glared at Jake.

"Oh, you can smell my anger? With those heightened senses you've been blessed with? The same ones that I, a shifter, also have?"

He started to open his mouth to say something then closed it again.

"I could smell him, too, Jake!"

"Who?"

"Malcolm!"

"Oh, I know, Cat."

Her glare intensified.

"Do I look weak to you, Jake? Because I'm not weak, Jake!"

"I know that, too."

"I'm a twelfth-degree black belt, Jake. Tae Kwon Do and Jujitsu! Which means I don't need a protector, Jake!"

Her voice echoed off the kitchen walls.

"Baby, I know…" He raised his eyebrows.

"Double black belts? Seriously? I didn't know that. I'm impressed and proud!" He took in a deep breath, released it slowly. "Look, baby. I know you can take care of yourself. But if this guy is a former Marine Scout Sniper, that makes him a very dangerous person."

"I don't need protection or to be controlled, Jake! Not by anyone. I refused to be controlled by him, and for damn sure I won't be controlled by you!" Her rage was almost at a boiling point again.

She watched Jake take another deep breath as he lowered his voice.

"Baby, I'm not trying to control you; I never will. But I will protect you at any and all costs. Did he ever tell you the details of his training or his job in the Corps?"

She did remember some of Malcolm's stories. And how detailed he talked about some of his training. But she thought he was just bragging to impress or intimidate her.

Jake explained what Malcolm's job was. The severe discipline he underwent. Most of those who attended that training dropped out because of the psychological pressure. In the field, some snapped. The thought of hunting another human became extremely distasteful. There were others who relished the hunt. Jake explained Malcolm's training consisted of being able to take out his target from nearly a mile away. And he would be long gone before the authorities showed up to the scene.

"Did you attend that training?"

"No, that was not my specialty."

Cathryn realized now she had no idea of what kind of man she'd dated. She began to understand how dangerous Malcolm was or could be. But that didn't mean she was going to become a victim and live in constant fear. Thinking back, she wondered if he'd been waiting for a friend. More than likely not. But that didn't matter. She wouldn't tolerate his bullshit anymore.

A cold chill ran up her spine as she stepped into Jake's arms. She leaned into him and laid her head against his chest. The chill slid away from her the tighter he held her. She heard his heartbeat slow as she slipped her hands up his back. She loved the feel of him. His heat surrounded her.

Wrapped in his arms, she relaxed more and became comfortable. Her wolf knew they needed to be protected by this alpha male, but the woman felt they didn't need protecting like some weak victim. His big arms felt fantastic. Electricity and heat moved through her body. Her core heat increased as Jake caressed her back. His hand moved up to the back of her head. Jake gently curled his hand into her hair, then gently pulled her head back. He raised her head to look at him. Cathryn was forced to look Jake directly in the eyes. The look he gave her let her know he meant business.

"Cat, baby, I will protect you no matter what. It's what I do. It's going to happen."

This dominant move did strange things to her. Her response was a natural reaction to Jake. Her eyes dilated, her breathing became heavy, almost panting. Cathryn melted into Jake's arms. Usually, this kind of behavior from any other man would have pissed her off, and then she would have dropped him where he stood. But from Jake, it excited her, aroused her with a clear intent that she would let him protect her, against her better judgment. Slowly he released her, kissed her forehead, and walked into the living room.

Cathryn's heartrate finally slowed, as did her breathing when Jake released her and walked into the living room. This man definitely got to her, very fast. She'd been so distracted by the whole Malcolm thing. She forgot why she walked into the kitchen in the first place after getting the dogs' food ready. Wine!

Wine bottle and glasses in hand, she stopped dead in her tracks as she walked into the living room. Jake's magnificent ass had her mesmerized. She couldn't take her eyes off him as he bent over in front of the fireplace. Round and firm enough to bounce a quarter off of. She licked her lips as his thick thigh muscles rippled through his jeans while he shifted his weight to move the logs into the fireplace. She loved how fit he was; that body did not come from working out in a gym. He had a natural hard body. She sent a quiet prayer of thank you to his parents and the United States Marines.

Sweat formed on her brow. The pooling in her panties increased. The convulsions in her pussy weren't helping at all. She damn near jumped out of her skin when he stood, turned, and looked directly into her eyes. He must have sensed her walk into the room because the smile he gave her showed he liked her thought about the wine.

"Hey."

"Hey." She had a guilty, apologetic look as she walked toward him.

"Jake, honey, I'm sorry about the way I reacted before. I just need you to understand how Malcolm tried so damn hard to control me while we were together. He wanted to dictate all aspects of my life, even the sex, which was terrible by the way. He seemed like he was about to get physical with me."

Which Malcolm did, but she was not going to tell Jake this, not yet.

"So, I had to break it off. After that, I put men out of my life for a while. I didn't want or need them. I was fine being independent and alone. Then you came along. And this…"

She gestured by waving her hand between herself and him.

"This is moving too fast for me. I can't help that little part of me panicked. I felt you were trying to do the same thing."

Jake took her in his arms, looked deep into her eyes.

"Look, baby. I understand, really I do. I promise that I will never try to control you. However, I will protect you! No matter the cost. My wolf and I are in complete agreement on this. Because, baby, Malcolm smells dangerous."

"But Malcolm's my problem, not yours."

"No. Malcolm's our problem now. And I'm not taking any chances with him around."

He held her chin between his forefinger and thumb. He raised her eyes to his.

"Understand?"

He stressed that last word, with his Alpha commanding tone and a look in his eyes. That tone meant he meant business. She knew that tone; her grandmother used it a lot when she was trying to defy her orders. He was being dominant again, which forced her to obey, but she didn't mind doing it at all.

"I understand. I should know better than to argue with a Jarhead."

"That will make life so much easier for the both of us." He gave her a devilish grin.

***

Jake wrapped her in his arms, nuzzled her neck. There was a tightening in his chest like nothing he'd ever felt before. An ache that, if something took her away, there would be a massive hole in his being, like half of his soul would be gone. She was his. He knew it. His wolf knew it. Now his soul knew it. She was the end of those long, cold, lonely nights in his house and his bed. He just needed to convince her and try not to freak her out.

She felt soft, warm in his arms. He trailed sweet kisses along her neck. She moaned, tilted her head back to give him better access. Slowly Jake caressed down her back to her backside. Her ass was soft but firm as he massaged her healthy globes. Oh, yeah, he was done being alone.

Chapter 14

Jake thought, '*That was easy!*'

As he snuck out of her bedroom, Cathryn looked so beautiful sound asleep. He hated to leave her, but he needed to find out what that asshole had been up to.

He put his clothes, jacket, and boots on at the bottom of the stairs. The dogs were in front of the fireplace. They jumped up and followed him out the door. He squatted down in front of them and whispered,

"Stay and protect the house."

He turned, walked toward the west fence, then he shifted. He cleared the fence in one sudden leap. He took off in a full run up the mountain toward the direction of that scent. A small amount of it still lingered in the air. After about a mile he stopped and shifted. There was a boot- print in the mud with leaf droppings that didn't belong in this region.

Jake curled his nose at the oily scent that still lingered. It came from the leaf droppings. That bastard brought his sniper rifle and put Cathryn in his crosshairs. Jake turned toward the direction of Cathryn's cabin. The next had a direct line of sight through her bay window in the kitchen. Uncontrollable rage coursed through his body. His wolf pushed hard and fast to the surface. Jake almost let him out. He was more than ready and willing to go on a berserker hunt.

"I'm gonna kill that son of a bitch!"

The wind shifted. Jake inhaled a sweet scent: lilac, jasmine, and female musk. Adrenaline rushed through his body. Jake prepared to attack the intruder. He whipped around, growled, and saw the most beautiful black wolf with deep amber eyes. She stood there staring at him. "Damn it, woman! Don't sneak up on me like that!" he snapped, still on his adrenaline/rage high.

The wolf shifted. Cathryn stood with her hands on her hips and smiled at him.

"You seriously thought you could sneak out of bed, let alone out of the house, and I wouldn't know it? That is too hilarious. What did you find?"

"Leaf droppings from his ghillie suit, and boot prints."

"His ghillie what?"

"Ghillie suit. It's a camouflage suit snipers use to blend into their surroundings. This is not made from the foliage of this area, so it was easy to spot."

He showed her a few leaves on the ground.

"What's the smell? It's kind of oily, like him."

"Gun oil. It's from his rifle. Fucker brought his weapon with him!"

Jake growled through gritted teeth. His wolf paced and snarled. They both wanted to rip Malcolm apart and bathe in his blood. Jake was having a hard time remaining in control of his beast. He hadn't felt rage like this in a long time.

***

A cold chill ran through Cathryn's body, followed by anger. The possibilities of what Malcolm could do to her or Patty filled her mind with dread. She squatted down and touched Malcolm's boot tracks. Her rage increased; the nerve of that asshole trying to turn her into his prey. She and her wolf were insulted. But Cathryn had to remain calm, in control to keep her head clear. She needed patience to not do anything stupid. Malcolm would make the first move, which would be his last.

Jake and Cathryn jumped the fence and shifted together when they arrived back at her cabin. Jake opened the door to let her and the dogs in then closed it behind them. After they toed off their boots and put their coats on the hooks by the door, they moved toward the pit. They stepped down, sat took a deep breath, then released at the same time. They looked at each other then laughed, but the tension still hung in the air.

"Jake, I thought about arguing with you for sneaking out to recon without me, but again why would I argue with a Jarhead!"

Jake turned his body toward her.

"Look, baby, I know I'm overprotective. That's not ever going to change. I care too much. All I ask is, please be patient with me on this?"

Cathryn turned towards him.

"I understand that you are overprotective, but you have to understand something about me since *this is* about me. I will not be treated like I'm some porcelain doll. I can handle any and all of life's disappointments. You will keep me in the loop, Mr. Carrington. You find out anything. I mean any…little…thing, you will let me know. Do you understand me? I will not be kept in the dark about anything, Jake! You get me, Marine?"

Jake's eyes widened in response to her last four words and smiled. What ran through his head she didn't know, but his response was, "Yes, ma'am! I know not to argue with a woman who can kick my ass."

Cathryn stood very slowly, then moved to stand in front of him. She straddled his feet, seductively spread her legs then lowered herself onto his lap. Cathryn placed her knees on either side of his hips, then put her hands on his chest. She rolled her hips to widen her legs, pushing her pelvis close to his. She felt his cock throb in his jeans while she rubbed her heat against him. Jake grabbed her hips. The pressure increased against her pussy. She hated the barrier of clothes between them.

"Now that we have established who the alpha female is, your next command, Marine, is to take me upstairs, rip off my clothes, and fuck me like the alpha male you are. You get me, Marine?"

Cathryn knew she used the right seductive, commanding voice as she felt his cock expand further. With a devilish grin, he willingly obeyed her command and responded with a very excited "Yes, ma'am!"

Jake grabbed the back of her head, took her lips in a hard, fervent kiss. He stood with her straddling his waist as if she weighed nothing. He stalked up the stairs two at a time then entered her bedroom. Jake kicked the door shut, then plopped her on the bed. He spread her legs with his knees, planted himself on top of her to devour her lips. Their tongues danced, tangled and teased each other. Cathryn felt his hands slowly move up her legs, ever so slowly up her body past her hips then under her sweater. Cathryn stopped his hands, broke their kiss.

"No, wait, I changed my mind."

She ignored the shocked look on Jake's face as she quickly moved from under him, then off the bed. Cathryn stood with her hands on her hips.

"My turn."

Jake didn't understand until she pushed him onto his back then climbed onto him.

"My turn to drive you wild tonight!"

He eyed her with curious, sensuous delight. He didn't know what she would do next, but he didn't have to wait long. She gave him the most delicious, seductive grin then kissed him passionately.

Cathryn grabbed the hem of his sweater, slowly, very slowly raised it up over his head, then pushed him back on the bed.

The look in his eyes as her hands caressed his chest was dark and sexy. He grabbed her hips and thrust his pelvis up toward her. Cathryn leaned on top of him, planted another passionate kiss then trailed more kisses down his shoulder, across his chest. She stopped at his nipples, licked, nibbled and sucked each one, going back and forth between them. He rewarded her with heavy breathing and a vise grip on her hips. Cathryn slowly moved her way down his body, but never took her eyes off his. She bent low, placed her lips on his stomach, licked just above his belt buckle. Slowly Cathryn continued to lick the trail of his hair from his belt up. She grinned when his breath hitched as she gradually unzipped his jeans.

***

If her goal was to drive him crazy with her slow pace, it worked. Jake's cock jumped several times from the anticipation of her destination. He'd dreamed of this all day, prayed she would service him, and she was. Jake made a silent prayer to the goddess for control until Cathryn had her way with him.

Cathryn looked up and met his gaze, smiled as if she heard his prayer. She moved her hands down his thighs. Cathryn sat back then removed his socks. Her eyes seemed to glow as she caressed her hands back up his legs. Cathryn hooked her fingers into the waistband of his jeans then pulled. Jake raised his hips as she slowly removed his jeans. He watched her lick her lips when his member became free from his jeans. She leaned back. He watched her chest rise and fall from her heaving breaths as she took his jeans with her to the floor.

Her hands slid up his legs. Heat trails followed in their wake. Jake watched her raise herself onto her knees as she stroked his thighs. His breathing increased to almost panting as she gently, reverently reached for his cock. Cathryn looked at his cock as if it was the most interesting thing in the world. He watched her every move as she licked her lips. It jumped in response. She touched, fondled his cock, licking it up and down with her eyes. Jake breathed slowly and tried to remain in control.

"Baby, what are you doing?"

"Admiring your cock."

She gently caressed him.

"I love the length of it, and the girth is magnificent. I can barely touch my fingers with my thumb. I adore the feel of it when you fill me, then stretch me while you're inside me."

His cock jumped again to reward her for her words. She licked the pre-cum from his mushroom. Jake gasped then rolled his head back as his hip involuntarily rolled up. Cathryn did that a couple more times, and Jake thought he would lose control.

He looked down at her as she wrapped her mouth around him, then slowly took him in. Jake closed his eyes, rolled his head back on the pillow, and thought about his dream. But this was so much better and hotter as she took him.

Her mouth felt amazing. Jake involuntarily rolled his hips, pushing his cock further past her luscious lips. Cathryn moaned, which sent electrical sensations throughout his body. He cried, then groaned in response to what she did to his cock and that made her smile. Jake felt her lips curl around him. Her mouth and hand had the perfect rhythm he liked. He looked down to see her cheeks hollowed as her grip tightened, which made him grunt more. Jake closed his eyes again as his head swam in ecstasy. His mind filled with emotions while his body felt sensations like never before. Never in his life had a woman pleasured him like this. The things she did to his cock amazed him and oh, goddess, that beautiful mouth of hers.

Before Jake knew what happened, his senses kicked up in intensity. Cathryn's arousal scent began to wreak havoc on his body. He could taste it. His skin perspired and felt sensitive to her touch. He opened his eyes; the waning moonlight filtered into the room so bright and beautiful. He looked down at Cathryn. The light sparkled off her hair like tiny bits of diamond dust. Her face, veiled by some of her ringlets, was the sexiest sight he had ever seen. Her eyes glowed with such intensity and focus on him. Tingling sensations swept through his body as the hair on his body stood on end. The emotions were so high. He didn't know if they were his or hers.

Jake was on the verge of exploding. He couldn't take any more.

"Aaahh, baby, I don't think I can hold on any longer. I need to be inside you now!!"

Jake sat up, pulled her from him, kissed her, then undressed her. Once all her clothes were off, he grabbed a condom from his wallet, sheathing himself just in time before Cathryn straddled him. In one smooth move, she pushed him back onto the bed again, then impaled herself on his cock. Jake sucked in a deep breath, closed his eyes tight and held her hips still.

"Oh shit, baby, don't move!! Please, goddess, baby, please don't move!!"

Panting hard, Jake barely caught his breath while he tried to remain in control.

Slowly, lightly, Cathryn dragged her nails down his chest. Her movements seemed to calm him. Jake relaxed a bit, but his cock was still rock-hard inside her. He opened his eyes, smiled up at her as his breathing slowed. Slowly Cathryn began to push down as he matched her rhythm. Jake closed his eyes; twinkling lights formed behind his lids. Jake swallowed hard, licked his lips as his breathing increased. Jake grabbed her by her wrists and held her as she undulated faster and faster. He wanted to flip her onto her back, then drive hard into her. But the view of her above him was breathtaking. His wolf was not very happy with her dominance. Jake reminded his wolf she wanted to be in charge at this time, it was her turn to pleasure him.

Her skin looked like smooth milk chocolate, almost caramel in the moonlight. Beads of sweat rolled down between her breasts that looked like honey. Jake licked his lips at the thought of licking it off her. Cathryn's moans of pleasure made him harder than he'd ever been before. The louder she moaned, the more laborious Jake pushed. The harder he pushed, the more she dug her nails into his chest. She held on and met him thrust for thrust.

Jake felt Cathryn was close to orgasm, her walls tightened and convulsed fiercely. He was about to lose control again but vowed he would not let go until she did. Then, as if on cue, Cathryn threw her head back, rocked hard against his hips and screamed, and her orgasm shook her whole body. The pleasure stamped on her face was marvelous. She partially shifted as she dug her claws into his chest, past his skin, into his thick chest muscles. Jake groaned from the pain but didn't give a damn about it as she rode out her orgasm. His lady marked him, and he would wear her claw marks with pride.

Jake grabbed her hips, pulled her close to him. One, two, three, four, five thrusts then Jake lost control, grunted, then pushed a deep to the hilt. He exploded deep inside her with such force he slid out of the condom and her.

They gazed into each other's eyes. Panting, sated, and smiling. Jake pulled her close to him. He threaded his fingers through her hair and massaged her scalp, while their lips met in a long, wet, passionate kiss.

He rolled her onto her back, still panting.

"Woman, you're going to be the death of me. I swear."

"Nope, I'm not done with you yet."

A panicked look crossed Cathryn's face. She sniffed then looked at her hands, then at his chest.

"Oh, my goddess! Baby, I'm so sorry!"

There wasn't a lot of blood, just a few drops on her nails and his chest, but enough to leave scars.

"It's okay, baby. I'm fine."

Jake left her spread-eagled on her bed. He went into her bathroom, threw away the condom, then cleaned his chest. He felt her concern. She was distraught that she'd clawed him. He smiled as he walked back into her bedroom. She looked relaxed as she lay there. He placed the warm cloth in between her legs to clean her as she spread her legs wider, then sighed and giggled.

"What are you giggling about?"

"Private joke. I might tell you someday…maybe."

Jake smiled down at her. "Fine, be that way. I'm too tired to argue with you about it."

Jake pulled the sheets back. Cathryn jumped up, turned her back toward him, then crawled to the other side. He swatted her butt; she squealed. Jake pulled her close to him then wrapped himself around her. He loved the way she fit into his body.

"Sorry about the claw marks, baby."

"Don't worry, baby. I love my marks."

He kissed her neck. They were the best mating marks any wolf would be proud to carry. His wolf loved the marks from their mate. The last thing Jake thought before he drifted off to sleep was he could get used to cuddling with this woman every night. That thought didn't scare him as much as he thought it would.

Chapter 15

The Mt. Charleston ski lodge was usually packed with tourists and locals. But tonight, it was quiet. Hardly anyone else was here. Patty sat at the far end of the bar alone, nursing her second Captain Morgan & Coke.

She sensed Cat had finally found someone who was going to be kind to her. She felt good emotions from Jake after their initial handshake. But something was wrong tonight; they were upset about something or someone earlier. She couldn't put her finger on it, but she'd find out once she arrived home.

She inhaled a familiar stench when she walked into the lodge earlier. Cat's ex-boyfriend had been here. What the hell was he doing on this side of town? She described him to Jerry, the bartender. He confirmed that the scumbag had definitely been here. Jerry told her everything Malcolm had done when he arrived, including what he drank. All the women he tried to hit on and how he failed miserably. She shook her head. That was like him to stalk her best friend and still try to pick up his next prey.

Jerry told her he asked a lot of questions about her and Cat. He told Malcolm what he wanted him to know. Jerry was a high school classmate of theirs. Still considered them good friends, because he knew all about Cathryn's ex and knew enough to keep anything significant from Malcolm.

Patty finished her drink, tipped Jerry, and thanked him for all his help. She stepped into her SUV and headed home. She felt relaxed. The drinks helped after a long night serving drinks to others. She sensed Cat and her contentment.

'So that's what happiness feels like.'

Nice was the only other word that came to her mind as she smiled the rest of the way up the mountain to home.

***

Feeling frustrated, Malcolm didn't get any information about Cathryn or her roommate from that bartender at the ski lodge. Getting her back was going to be harder than he thought. Just a little setback that wasn't going to deter him from his goal. It would be worth it to literally bring that bitch to her knees. He needed to change his tactics a bit. She was with that male who arrived at the cabin with her. He was the same one who gave her roses and hugged her at the lounge bar.

He had the perfect view of her through the crosshairs of his scope. He saw inside her kitchen through the bay window from his nest earlier tonight. He had to do something about those damn dogs. They must have scented him when the wind changed. They faced his direction when Cathryn arrived. There was no way she and that guy could have known he was there; they were too stupid. He knew he was a better hunter than anyone in the Corps. He'd placed first on his team in training school. He had to think of a way of getting rid of the dogs, then the roommate and the new boyfriend.

***

As they ate breakfast, Cathryn realized her connection to Jake deepened. Not just on the empathic emotional level, but her instinctive level. The more they made love, the more in depth she sensed him. They talked about when the connection started. She told him it had to have been before the kiss on the hand. Sometimes she could smell his scent every now and then depending on what area she worked at that time.

She listened as Jake talked about his family. He'd lost his parents at a young age, too. She heard, felt his anguish when Jake spoke about his mother. How he felt after she took her life. Jake felt abandoned, and then anger that turned into self-destruction and his rebelliousness toward his grandfather and his uncle. He had stopped his daily meditation. He almost lost control of his beast a few times. The berserker rage became virtually addicting. To be able to channel that anger felt powerful.

Jake shared with Cathryn his relationship with 'what's her name.' The woman in the magazine article. They dated for three years after high school. He thought she loved him for him. He was set to propose when he went to their family jeweler to pick out her ring. She had already been there and chose the most expensive one. She told the jeweler he could afford it.

After he confronted her, that's when his wolf and his instincts slammed into him like a two by four to the back of his head. The scent that rolled off her made his stomach turn and skin crawl. The stench of greed overwhelmed him. He broke it off then. But she tried her damnedest to convince him she loved him only for him.

The more she talked, the more pissed off he became. He needed to clear his head, so he went to a bar for a drink. Or, in his case, a lot of drinks. Some guy made a mistake and accidentally bumped into him at the bar. The next thing he remembered was his uncle and RL chased him through the forest and tranquilized him with a dart.

The next day his uncle gave him an ultimatum. Either go to jail for the extensive damage to the bar or join the Marines. He needed to learn to channel his rage. Jonathan spoke to the owner and convinced him to drop all the charges against Jake and paid for all of the damages he caused.

He told Cathryn the night before he left for boot camp, he went on a hike through the woods in his human form. He felt distraught, confused, and still angry.

"This may sound weird, but I saw my mother."

Cathryn's eyes became wide. Because she knew exactly what he was talking about.

"You did? How did she appear to you?"

"It was at night. At first, a mist formed in my path and then the mist almost solidified."

"Did she speak to you?"

"Yes. She apologized for leaving me alone. That was no excuse for what she did. But she missed my dad so much. The loss of his connection was such a huge hole in her soul, she couldn't recover. But she knew I would be taken care of by my uncle and grandfather. That's when most of my internal rage began to recede."

And it worked. He found the perfect way to control his beast and himself. The Corps taught him discipline, and he also remembered his meditations.

"I would either be in jail or dead if not for my uncle and grandfather. I owe them so much."

Cathryn touched his hand. He wove his fingers into hers. She remembered her grief when her parents died in that plane crash. She thanked the goddess for her grandmother. She would have gone down a path of destruction as well.

She also understood how his mother must have felt. Her connection to Jake had strengthened to the point that she felt his presence in her being all the time. She didn't know, if anything were to happen to Jake, if she could or would survive his loss.

She learned they liked the same movies. She told Jake about the movie she started to watch the night he kissed her hand. She did not want to watch any mushy love story or any film with too many love scenes in it. He confessed he watched the same movie for the very same reasons.

Patty walked in, headed to the coffee maker. "What's so funny?"

Cathryn told her the story; they all laughed.

"I didn't hear you come in last night," Cathryn said.

"No? Well, I sure heard you two!" Patty winked.

Cathryn returned her wink as Jake fixed Patty a plate of eggs and bacon with diced potatoes. Patty thanked Jake and dug into the dish.

She looked at Cathryn. "Who cooked?"

"Me," Jake replied with a big wolf grin.

Patty looked at him, nodded her head.

"You're right, Cat. He is damn good at what he does. No wonder you're all smiles this morning."

She winked again.

"We should definitely keep this one around for a while, Cat."

Cathryn agreed then asked her about her night. Patty gave her the rundown. She told them she stopped at the ski lodge and Malcolm had been there.

Cathryn felt Jake's energy change. She didn't have to look at him. She immediately caressed his arm to calm him. Patty's story of Malcolm's attempted flirting with the women and how he failed miserably put somewhat of a smile on Jake's face. He cleared the dishes as Patty finished her story.

Cathryn told Patty that Malcolm had been near the property, about a mile up the mountain. Jake finished with the sniper's nest and that he brought his weapon. Cathryn felt a chill from Patty when Jake told her about Malcolm's specialty in the Marines.

“So, what are we going to do? Should you call the police?” Patty asked.

“We don’t have any real evidence to prove that he was on the property. Just near it,” Jake said. “Just because we could smell him, and the dogs’ reaction to the direction he was at, won’t hold water in their eyes. Except to those on the force who are shifters like us,” he finished.

“Yep, and just because he showed up at the casino wouldn’t mean anything either,” Cathryn said.

“Wait! What! What do you mean he was at the casino?!” Patty shouted.

“Yeah, he was there. Told me he was waiting for a friend, which I know now was bullshit,” Cathryn said.

“That’s stalking! He was at the ski lodge, which is way out of the way for him. He lives completely on the other side of town. He asked Jerry a lot of questions about us.” Patty paused. “No, wait, he could lie and say that he was waiting for a friend there, too.”

“Yes, besides, we don’t want him to know we’re on to him. Not yet anyway. He’s hunting and thinks we ‘re too stupid to know,” Jake said, then looked at Cathryn. “Baby, did you tell him about your abilities?”

“No! I made sure he knew about my self-defense, which I stressed a lot in the last month of our relationship. And I had to demonstrate… once.”

“What do you mean, you had to demonstrate?” Jake’s voice rose a couple of decibels.

Cathryn felt his anger, then quickly walked toward him. She placed her hands on his chest where her marks were.

"He tried to get physical with me by grabbing my arm. I broke his hold. I placed my thumb against the back of his hand then pressed down to hold him in place."

Cathryn felt Jake's anger recede when she finished.

"He obviously didn't remember that I could do a lot more than that to him."

Jake took two long deep breaths as his anger dissipated more.

"Okay, in the meantime we'll let Malcolm believe that we're not aware of his silent stalking. My uncle and I have family and friends in the police department as well as the D.A.'s office. I will make sure that any and all investigations stay quiet."

Patty finished her coffee, put her cup in the sink, and gave Jake a see you later wave as she left the kitchen. Cathryn walked Jake to the door. As he put on his jacket she grabbed his lapel and pulled him down and planted a wet, passionate kiss on his lips.

Jake grabbed her by her waist and responded with equal passion.

"Mmmmm…baby, we get this started again, and I won't be leaving."

He growled in a low sexy voice against her lips. She smiled and nodded her head in agreement.

"Oh, by the way, baby, my uncle planned a small bar-b-que this coming weekend. He'd love it if you could join us. He wants to meet you. In fact, he stressed that I should bring you. And when I say stressed, I mean that he will do severe bodily harm to me if I show up without you. Nothing compared to the beautiful marks you left on my chest by the way."

He rubbed his chest with an exaggerated look of terror on his face.

She rolled her eyes.

"Fine, if I have to save your life from your uncle, I'll go. Lucky for you and your body I'm off. I will be there."

With a heavy sigh he smiled.

He smiled, kissed her, swatted her on her butt, then walked out the door. Jake stopped just outside the doorway, scanned the area, then inhaled.

"Pine…sage…dogs. All is well."

Cathryn closed the door, and a wave of panic hit her. Patty ran down the stairs.

"What's wrong?"

"Huh? Oh, nothing. Jake just told me his uncle is having a bar-b-que and wants to meet me."

"Okay, so his uncle wants to meet you. What's the problem?"

"I have absolutely nothing to wear!" She threw her hands up, intentionally exaggerating her problem.

"Cat, it's a bar-b-que; you can wear jeans, t-shirt, and sneakers for goddess' sake!"

"Yeah, but you know me. I always want an excuse to go shopping."

"I'm done with you." Patty walked up the stairs to her bedroom.

Chapter 16

Malcolm looked at the folder of information he received about Jake and Jonathan Carrington. He remembered the new boyfriend, Staff Sergeant Jake Carrington. He never knew his first name, but he was one of the Recon idiots who screwed up the information that caused his dishonorable discharge from the Corps. Malcolm learned that Jake's family had influential friends in high places as well, but vengeance was his right. He would have his day or year. However long it took.

There was another woman from his recent past, who was sort of like Cathryn. What was her name? Oh yeah, Brenda. She thought she was strong and independent. He always started his hunt being charming and attentive. Malcolm told Brenda everything she wanted to hear which made her comfortable with him; he liked to use that tactic, which gave her a false sense of security. Then slowly he shifted and whittled her down until she was what he wanted her to be: weak, compliant, and entirely dependent on him. Very slowly Malcolm broke her will. He gradually started with mental abuse, then verbal abuse. He told her how inadequate she was, that she was stupid, and she was nothing without him.

The perfect part was poor Brenda never saw it coming. He talked her out of going back to school to get her degree in business. Malcolm purposely sabotaged every thought, every hope and dream she had. She actually tried to stand up for herself; he gave her a stern look, slowly walked toward her, and invaded her space which made her shrink into herself in fear.

He kept track of her phone calls to let her know he could find her anywhere. He called her work every two hours to check on her; he backed off just a little because she'd gotten into trouble with her supervisor. So, he started to take her to and from work only to remind her he was in charge.

He escalated his power and became physical. He'd grab her, push her and even backhanded her a few times, which gave him a hard-on. He felt powerful knowing he could control her, and she never fought back which he also loved. And he reminded her that every time he was upset, it was her fault not his.

She started putting on more cover-up to hide the bruises on her face and body. Malcolm smiled and remembered the thrill it gave him for her to be so afraid to look at him wrong. He became bored when he finally broke her down to nothing. He eventually left her, to find other prey to start the ritual over again.

But Cathryn was mentally stronger than he anticipated. She told him she had martial arts training. He didn't think Cathryn was physically strong enough to break his hold on her arm, but she did. She surprised him. He sported a black eye and swollen lip for a while. That would be the last time she humiliated him. He knew what he had to do. Hunt her like prey and find her weakness, then she would be at his mercy.

Chapter 17

A twenty-foot-wide sign that displayed the name 'Spanish Hills' greeted them as they turned up the three-lane driveway. Jake stopped his truck at the security gatehouse, where an armed security officer stood in the doorway of a glass booth. He watched Jake swipe his key card at the scanner. The gate officer nodded to him as the gate arm lifted, then Jake proceeded to enter the lavish community.

Beautifully paved roads led from the gatehouse; palm trees lined both sides. Cathryn noticed a massive building made of glass surrounded by a manicured lawn. Jake told her that was the Spanish Hill Country Club. Seasonal parties were held there, as well as debutante balls for the daughters of the Spanish Hills elite.

Cathryn was in awe of the vast estates and the well-kept lawns as they drove on. Jake told her there were different levels of the gated community. She noticed the higher they drove, the more significant, more elaborate the homes became, as opposed to the ones on the lower end.

The exterior designs were like nothing she'd ever seen before; each mansion uniquely designed, nothing like the track homes in the rest of the Las Vegas communities.

Jake turned into a driveway of a huge home.

"Wow! This is where you come from? You grew up here?"

"Here? No, baby. My uncle built this almost three years ago. I grew up with my grandfather in a small house in town after my parents died. But I did spend a lot of time with my uncle at his other home before he sold it."

She looked open-mouthed at the size of the house Jake parked in front of.

He helped her out of the truck, took her hand as they walked up the steps. Cathryn's jaw dragged the ground as Jake strolled right in with her behind him. Her mouth became dry, and her eyes grew wider as they stepped into the vestibule.

The interior design was beautiful. The floors were polished white marble with streaks of gold. The walls were eggshell white trimmed with earth tone brown. The great room was past the entryway; to her left was an enormous gas fireplace outlined in the same white marble tiles as the floor. The decorations and furnishings didn't look like a man had chosen them. Everything matched, flowed. She wondered if his uncle hired someone to decorate for him. But whoever designed it did a fantastic job.

Pictures and statues of wolves were everywhere in various colors. On the mantelpiece were photos of a young boy, which had to be Jake. There were pictures of family members as well as wedding pictures of couples. A newer one must be of Jakes' parents. His mother looked so happy and beautiful in her dress. Jake was the spitting image of his father.

'It would have been nice to have met them both.'

Over the fireplace hung a huge portrait of an older gentleman. His features looked a lot like Jake's, except he had long hair that was completely gray. Cathryn couldn't help but stare as she looked up at the picture over the fireplace. She smiled when Jake walked up behind her, slid his arms around her waist.

Jake nuzzled Cathryn's neck. "What are you smiling at?"

"Now I know where you get your good looks from."

"And me!" came a voice from their right.

She turned around to see who must have been Jake's uncle walk through a set of French doors. He stopped in front of Jake, gave him a big hug, and then slapped him on his back.

"Hello, son. Who do we have here?"

“Uncle, this is Cathryn. Cathryn, this is my Uncle Jonathan,” Jake said

“It’s a pleasure to meet you, my dear. How are you doing?” Jonathan asked

“Fine, thank you; it’s a pleasure to meet you, too,” Cathryn responded

She held her hand out to shake but Jonathan took her hand, slowly turned her palm down, then kissed the back of her hand. The same wow factor happened; electricity flowed through her, but not as intense as when she first met Jake.

Jonathan explained that the portrait was of his father, Jake’s grandfather.

“So, this is the one who’s been giving you sleepless nights and has your mind wandering off all the time? She’s more beautiful than you said.”

He never took his eyes off of her.

Caught in Jonathan’s gaze, Cathryn felt a hot blush on her cheeks. Jonathan’s alpha presence electrified the air around her. His direct eye contact commanded her full undivided attention, the same as when she first touched Jake’s hand. Not that she was attracted to his uncle but respected his authority.

“Yeah, yeah, knock it off, you sly old wolf.”

Jake took her hand back from his uncle’s.

His uncle laughed at him.

“Welcome princess. I want you to make yourself at home. Come this way; the party is in the backyard.”

She followed Jonathan out the French doors with Jake right behind her, onto a huge patio. Cathryn's bottom jaw hit the ground again.

"Wow, your uncle calls this a small bar-b-que? He goes all out for a small bar-b-que."

Several dozen people attended this 'little' bar-b-que. Some people she had seen in the newspapers, magazines, and on television.

The backyard was more like a vast field that stretched at least a quarter of a football field in length. High trees lined both sides of the area with walls at least ten feet tall outside them. An Olympic-size swimming pool was to the right of the patio with a tennis court to the left. Propane heaters lined the patio's perimeter. Which was a good idea since the temperature was in the mid-fifties in January. Jake introduced her to most of the guests he knew. They ran into the Clark County sheriff; Jake told her he was an old friend of the family.

They continued toward the bar-b-que pit for some food. Jake's uncle apparently spared no expense when he threw a party. Large buffet tables were filled with ribeye steaks, beef ribs, corn on the cob, and salads of all kinds. The pit itself was full of steaks, ribs, and other meats. A man dressed in Levi's, a plaid shirt, and wearing cowboy boots attended the meat on the grill.

They gathered their plates when Cathryn asked Jake, "Seriously, no paper plates?"

The plates were not like the ones at the Casino's buffet but the nonbreakable Chinet kind. There was no plasticware either, actual silverware. They grabbed their plates, cutlery, and started with the ribeye's, salad, then drinks.

"Nope, my uncle does not believe in paper or plastic anything at a party, especially a bar-b-que."

They found an open table and then dove into their food. Cathryn felt that *'Oh my goddess'* orgasm feeling again while she chewed her steak.

"It tastes almost as good as your cooking."

"We Carrington men don't do anything in a small way. Our family motto is if you're going to do anything, do it big."

He leaned into her ear.

"And that includes making love to a beautiful woman." Then he kissed her cheek.

"Well, I can attest to that." Cathryn smiled.

Jonathan cleared his throat as he walked up to the table with his plate and joined them.

"That family motto goes back a long way to our Norwegian roots. Are you having a good time, Cathryn?"

"Yes, I'm having a wonderful time. Thank you for inviting me."

"My pleasure, I'm glad to hear that. So... you two...what's going on?"

Jake and Cathryn looked at each other, then at Jonathan with surprised looks.

"Nothing much, Uncle. Why do you ask?"

Cathryn watched Jonathan. His face was down toward his plate of food. He didn't raise his head, just his eyes.

"I know something's wrong. I can feel it. As if you could try to hide something, anything from me. Plus, I can smell it... on the both of you. Talk to me, son, and I mean now. What's wrong?"

There was an Alpha command, the likes of which she had not heard since her grandmother sometimes used it on her years ago. Jake was compelled to answer. He told his uncle the whole story about Cathryn's ex. From the time he showed up at the casino, to the bar at the ski lodge. To where they tracked him on the mountain close to her cabin.

"Uncle, we don't want to alarm him just yet; he doesn't know we're on to him. So, we need to keep this as low-key as possible."

"I agree."

He looked at Jake then at Cathryn.

"So, he's a scout-sniper?"

They both nodded yes.

"Jake, do you know him?"

"Not personally. But I think we served in Afghanistan around the same time."

***

Jonathan was not pleased about this at all. He just met Cathryn and liked her. He sensed she was a shifter and a good woman. Her scent was perfect for his nephew. Not a bit of greed on her. He already thought of her as the daughter he never had. Mostly because she put a smile on his nephew's face. She was someone who would put Jake in his place now and then.

Jonathan had heard enough.

"I'm going to have both the department heads of security and surveillance know about this Malcolm person. Then pass that information on to their people. If they see him, just notify their shift supervisors. Do not approach until told to do so."

"Uncle, I was thinking we could call in some favors to get some background on Malcolm. Just to see what kind of person we're up against."

"Great idea. You handle that."

***

Cathryn sat in silence next to Jake. She listened to the men talk about her life as if she wasn't there. She was not happy with the situation. This was her problem. Malcolm was her problem. Not anyone else's to fix. The two men stopped their conversation, and then looked at Cathryn at the same time. Jonathan placed a hand on hers on the table.

"What's wrong, princess?"

His touch was warm. It relaxed her a little bit, just a little bit.

"Look, Mr. Carrington," she started to say, but he stopped her in mid-sentence.

"Please, call me Jonathan."

"Okay, Jonathan. I don't feel comfortable having other people take care of a problem that is mine. Like I told Jake last week, Malcolm is my problem and I will take care of him. The only reason I let Jake handle it this far is because he would continue to hound me if I didn't."

Jonathan looked at his nephew with pride and smiled.

"Well, princess, from this point on, we both will hound you if you don't let us help you. It's a Carrington male trait. Besides, no self-respecting Marine would ever leave a lady in distress."

Cathryn rolled her eyes, leaned against Jake.

"Oh, great goddess. Just what I need in my life! Another Jarhead!"

Jake put his arm around her shoulder, and then kissed the top of her head. Jonathan smiled as he leaned back in his chair.

"So, are you two going to spend the night? It's a long drive back up the mountain. Jake, your room is always ready for you."

Jake looked at Cathryn. She shrugged her shoulders and smiled.

"Sure, why not."

The bar-b-que lasted well past midnight. Cathryn enjoyed herself hobknobbing with Las Vegas' rich and elite. Some guests asked her what she did for a living. She told them, not ashamed of her present career choice. Some raised their eyebrows but dared not say anything negative. It was obvious that she was a close friend of Jonathan's nephew. All in all, she had a great time.

As she lay in Jake's bed, she was pissed. The word 'victim' was neither in her vocabulary nor part of her persona. But she was no fool either; she understood how dangerous Malcolm was. But getting Jake's uncle involved was making her more uncomfortable and pissed off.

Chapter 18

Cathryn had a great time with Jake and his uncle last week. But today she had an uneasy feeling. Something seemed off. She sensed someone watched her. But she couldn't pinpoint the direction. Mostly she felt it when she walked into or out of the casino. Her senses hadn't picked up anyone in particular, but her instincts told her someone was out there.

She felt comfortable in the casino. She thought about going to the courthouse to get a restraining order as Patty suggested. But there wasn't enough evidence that he harassed her, let alone stalked her. She hated this feeling of helplessness, mainly since she wasn't.

This was Malcolm's head game. He wanted her to feel completely helpless. Make her believe she was alone and had nowhere to go or anyone to help her. She didn't need anyone's help, but he didn't know that. She and Jake were already five steps ahead of him. He'd trip up, and when he did he'd be in the middle of a major shit storm.

Cathryn walked through her usual slot areas with a fake smile pasted on. She felt something was terribly wrong. Patty wasn't working today. She told her she was going to get a mani/pedi, then do some grocery shopping. And that she'd be home around six.

Cathryn received a text from Patty at five, asking if she needed anything special from the store. Cat responded: 'nothing special. Just don't forget the milk, eggs and dog food.' Patty replied with a smiley emoji. Cathryn seemed a little at ease because she'd heard from Patty, but she still sensed something was wrong. Something terrible was either happening or was going to happen.

***

Patty finished all her errands and was on her way back toward the mountain. She sensed someone followed her, but when she looked in her rearview mirror no one was there. She turned left up to the mountain from the highway and saw a truck behind her. It kept enough distance, so she couldn't make out the license plate, even with her shifter vision. Too much dust billowed up behind her. She couldn't make out the make or model of the vehicle either.

Patty turned into the driveway, pulled up to the gate. As soon as she stepped out of her SUV, something hit her in the thigh. She felt a sting, and then her vision became blurry. A figure walked toward her from across the road. She knew immediately who it was before she completely blacked out.

'Son of a bitch. I didn't even smell him.'

***

Cathryn texted Patty several times between 6:30 and 7:00, with no response. It was not like Patty to not respond at all. Cathryn could tell something was horribly wrong; she felt it in her being.

Cathryn continued her rounds through High-Limit slots, dropping off drink orders. She felt something sharp stab her in her thigh and nearly collapsed. She looked at her leg, but nothing was there. She knew immediately it was Patty; even at this distance, she knew something had happened to her. Patty was in serious trouble.

Cathryn walked into Roger's office on her break. She told him something was wrong at home, and she needed to leave work early. She said she tried to contact Patty but received no response. Cathryn didn't tell him precisely what was wrong. He told her he couldn't let her leave because they were short-handed. He felt terrible, but he couldn't allow her to go home early. She walked back to the station, frustrated. She felt helpless and began to panic. She decided to go over Roger's head. She texted Jake. Cathryn knew he was in his office today.

***

An all-consuming emotion of dread washed Jake just before he received a text from Cathryn. He raced down to the casino floor to find her. He saw her pacing back and forth in front of the lounge bar like a caged animal.

“What’s wrong, baby?”

She was damn near in a full-blown panic; he felt it.

“Jake, something’s wrong with Patty. I can feel it. I’ve texted her. She’s not answered back. It has been over forty-five minutes since her last response. This isn't like her. She always, always texts me back.”

Cathryn looked around, then lowered her voice.

“I know something is wrong; I felt a sting in my leg and know it’s her. Something has happened to her. She told me she would be home around 6:00. It’s now after 7:00 and still no answer. I can’t leave because we’re short-handed, but I need to do something!”

Her fear and panic increased as they talked.

“Let me call my friend, RL. He can ride up there to see what’s happening. Don’t worry, baby. We’ll find out what’s going on. I promise.”

He hugged her then kissed her forehead. Jake turned back toward the offices. On his way he sent RL a text.

Chapter 19

Jake stared at the computer screen in his office. What he saw nauseated him. They were able to get a lot of information on Malcolm from their connections at the police department. The military information wasn't new to him. But what Jake found most disgusting was the sealed records of domestic violence. There were pictures of women battered, bruised. All that information had been covered up.

The police reports showed Malcolm had at least six charges of assault and battery brought against him in the past ten years. With zero arrests because either Malcolm paid them off, scared them into silence, or the women just disappeared. The police photos of the women he abused were terrible, which ate at Jake's core. Rage filled him the more he read on this asshole. His anger peaked to a dangerous level at the fact that this asshole was at one time with his woman. And what he thought he might try to do to her now. Which brought his wolf close to the surface.

Jake closed the folders, shut down his computer. A text message came in, he thought was from RL. It was Robert, and then another one almost at the same time came in from Alex. They knew something was wrong with him and wanted to see if he was okay. Jake responded to them. He told them things were happening, but would call them later as soon as he was able to.

That feeling of dread washed over him again, this time much worse. He locked the folder in his desk drawer. He raced down to the casino floor to find Cathryn. But he was too late. She had already left the station to clock out, according to one of the bartenders at the lounge bar. Jake went to the bar manager's office. Roger told him she clocked off work then left. He ran through the casino toward the parking garage. He had to get to her first to protect her from that maniac.

***

Cathryn drove home as fast as she could. She had tightness in her chest and felt in her bones that Patty was in trouble. She barreled up the mountain at top speed. Her SUV kicked up dust, rocks, and debris. She finally made it home. She took the turn into her driveway a little too fast. She barely missed sliding into Patty's SUV and almost hit the fence. Patty's driver's side door was still open. But what she saw in the yard stopped her heart cold.

She barely put her SUV in park before she jumped out, without closing her door. She ran toward the fence, jumped over it and ran toward the middle of the yard, only to stop dead in her tracks.

"No!!!"

Her dogs were on the ground, lying on their sides. Cathryn didn't have time to check them when something bit her on her neck. She swatted at what she thought was a bug. She reached to the back of her neck and realized it was a dart. She blinked her eyes, turned around, and saw him.

"You fucking son of a bitch!"

Then her world went dark.

***

Jake drove like a madman up the highway. He took the left turn a little too sharp and damn near skidded off into a ditch. He felt a sharp sting on the back of his neck, like an insect bite. He touched the back of his neck, pulled his hand away to see if there was any blood or a stinger. He felt weird, not dizzy, but panicked. Panic washed over him then it was gone. He realized it came from Cathryn.

Chapter 20

Cathryn tried to open her eyes. Her vision blurred, and she had a massive headache. She tried to move but had a hard time with it. Gradually her vision began to clear. She realized she was in the middle of her barn. Her hands were tied behind her to one of the main supports in the barn. She was on her knees, leaning forward.

That familiar stench of Malcolm hit her hard, which caused her to gag. She almost lost the contents of her stomach. Her shoulders ached from the position she'd been in while unconscious.

She groaned from the pain and almost gagged from Malcolm's scent. Slowly she stood to her feet. Her legs were wobbly, her vision cleared a little bit, but her head still pounded. The drug began to wear off. The foggy haze quickly lifted as her vision cleared more.

"Well, hello, my dear. I'm so glad you're finally awake," Malcolm snarled. He stalked toward her slowly as if he had hunted and captured her with all the confidence in the world.

Cathryn struggled to stand, to keep both feet planted beneath her. The more she moved, the worse her headache raged.

"Malcolm. What the fuck do you want?!" she demanded between breaths.

Malcolm stood directly in front of her as her legs finally became steady under her weight. She scrunched up her nose as his stench rolled off him. Cathryn swallowed the bile that rose in her throat.

'That's what crazy smells like.'

Malcolm grabbed her by the back of her hair, fisted it tight and tilted her face, forcing her to look at him. She winced as the pain in her head became ten times worse.

"Well, my dear, I thought that was obvious. I want you back. And I will have you back."

He released her hair with a jerk then walked away.

"You see, you humiliated me. I was trying to teach you a lesson when you attacked me."

"I attacked you? Malcolm, you were angry and grabbed me first. And I warned you about putting your hands on me. I told you never to bother me again!"

Cathryn struggled to move her hands. Whatever was around her wrists cut into her skin.

"Don't bother trying to break free. Those are military-grade zip-ties. You're not going anywhere unless I say so!"

She stopped moving for just a moment.

"I was only trying to tell you that you need me. You need me to take care of you. Your life was so chaotic and needed order. And that's why you need me now. I was not prepared that time. You just caught me by surprise that time."

Cathryn was still a little light-headed. She shook her head a little which sent jolts of pain through her head.

Breathing heavily, she growled, "And the only way you can subdue a strong woman is by drugging her? Well, Malcolm, that just makes you weak."

Malcolm backhanded her across her cheek, which snapped her head to her left and connected with the pole behind her.

Cathryn groaned, the pounding in her head increasing. Spots formed behind her eye-lids. She dropped her head to clear it. She raised her head again, but he never moved away from her. Her wolf pushed toward the surface, but Cathryn controlled her. Her rage was under control for the moment. Slowly she raised her head to glare at him.

"You need me to teach you a few fucking lessons. You need to understand who the fuck is in charge. And I'm going to enjoy pounding those lessons into you every second until you get the fucking point!"

Malcolm raised his right hand to backhand her again. Cathryn flattened her back against the pole, lifted both legs, then kicked out with both feet with surprising speed. She connected with his midsection.

Malcolm flew backward onto the ground, slid across the barn floor, bounced off the barn doors fifteen feet away, then rolled toward her. Cathryn partially shifted her hands, used her middle claw, and ripped through the zip-ties with ease. Her spirit animal's self-preservation instincts kicked in with such tremendous force, Malcolm didn't know what hit him.

Cathryn watched him shake his head. He grunted in pain. Malcolm looked at Cathryn with astonishment. She guessed he couldn't believe a woman could use that much force in a kick. He apparently forgot about her martial arts training.

He tried to stand up, but before he could regain his bearings she ran toward him and side- kicked him in his midsection again, which sent him flying. He flipped sideways over and over, then smashed through the barn doors. He landed outside with a crash on the debris. The wind was completely knocked out of him.

Cathryn ran outside as Malcolm flopped around on the ground and tried to stand. She kicked him in his face which sent him flying onto his back, hard. He moaned as he tried to fight unconsciousness.

"Malcolm, I warned you I was the last bitch on this earth to fuck with!" she growled.

She stood in a side fighting stance, her fists at the ready just below eye level. Her weight balanced on her back leg. She refused to take her eyes off of him.

She heard a vehicle pull into the driveway. Out of the corner of her eye, the black truck she recognized skidded to a halt. Quickly she looked back as Jake ran toward her. She kept her eyes on Malcolm as she back stepped toward Jake, then turned toward him. Jake grabbed her, wrapped his arms around her, and held her close.

"Baby! Are you okay?" His voice shook.

"Yea, I'm great now. Did you find Patty?"

"Yeah, RL texted me. He found her. She was in a cave just a few of miles up the road, tied up."

***

Malcolm, still on the ground, couldn't believe that a woman could drop him like that. A fucking woman! His vision cleared slightly. He saw them holding each other. That bitch humiliated him for this last time. Fuck teaching her a lesson.

He moved slowly—very, very slowly. Malcolm inched ever so slightly onto his knees. He reached behind his back, pulled his 9mm Beretta, aimed, then fired.

Malcolm watched what unfolded and felt triumphant. But before he took aim to take out the boyfriend, the man morphed into a massive black beast as he fired another round. The bullet whizzed past the creature. Didn't even graze him—some scout sniper he was.

The last thing Malcolm saw was a black blur with emerald green eyes that glowed and white fangs that dripped saliva as it barreled down on him. He didn't have time to react let alone scream as those teeth sank into his throat, crushed, then ripped out his flesh.

Then the pain became more than his mind could handle. Darkness swept him into oblivion.

***

After being examined by the paramedics, Cathryn sat on the back bumper of one of the EMT trucks. She wore a sling on her left arm while Jake wore one on his right. Jake stood beside her as he gave his report to the sheriff. Cathryn replayed the surreal scene in her mind again:

She never heard the shot but felt the sudden pain as the bullet hit her in her left shoulder blade. She jerked and screamed as the bullet ripped through her.

She slumped against Jake and slid down into his arms. She saw the fear in Jake's eyes as he lay her on the ground. Blood oozed out of a small hole in Jake's chest; that terrified her more than her own pain. She raised her hand to his chest as tears streamed down her cheeks. She watched the fear in Jake's eyes instantly replaced by rage. Once she was on the ground, she watched him shift in the blink of an eye. She remembered her grandmother talking about berserker rage. During that time the spirit animal became a beast whose size increased by ten. But to see it in person was amazing. Jake's wolf was bigger than any she had ever seen before, and magnificent.

She listened as Jake told the Clark County sheriff about the disembowelment of Malcolm. The sheriff and paramedics were shifters themselves, which was why Jake spoke so openly about the situation.

The sheriff knew all about Malcolm and his family's shady past, but could not do anything about it since they were out of his jurisdiction.

Animal Control was called there to check on the dogs. They told her Malcolm hadn't killed them. He just shot them with tranquilizers. They guessed to keep them out of his way. Cathryn breathed a sigh of relief, then a bigger sigh when Patty and RL arrived through the tree line.

Epilogue

Three weeks later

After being released from the hospital, Cathryn recuperated at Jake's house. He insisted with his damn alpha command tone. She stayed in the hospital for forty-eight hours. She had a private room where she could shift to heal her gunshot wound. Only a tiny scar remained.

She and Patty spoke on the phone every day, just to check on each other. Patty told her that she called their veterinarian to double-check the dogs. Sasha was pregnant and would give birth to seven pups around late March. Sasha, the puppies, and the other dogs were healthy.

Cathryn informed Patty that Jake took excellent care of her. But he drove her batshit crazy. It had been three weeks since she was shot. He wouldn't let her get out of bed to do anything, only to take a shower.

"Patty, this man has not touched me since we've been home. He says he worried he might lose control and be too rough with me."

"I think you're being a little overdramatic, Cat." Patty laughed

"This shit's not funny, Patty. I'm frustrated and extremely horny."

***

Alex and Robert came by almost every day to visit Jake and Cathryn to check on them. They both boarded the next flights to Las Vegas as soon as they felt Jake's pain from being shot. They called several times and left several messages. Finally, they reached RL on his cell, who told them what happened.

Jake made a point to find things to do outside to release his sexual tension. He missed making love to Cat but loved being curled up next to her every night, then waking up with her in his arms every morning. But her scent drove him crazy. It became stronger every day. It seemed to permeate the entire house now. But he vowed to stay in control. There was no way he was going to take any chances with her health.

He hadn't lost control of his berserker in a long time. He didn't know if it would happen again so soon. Or if he would lose control again while making love to Cathryn.

Jake worked up a severe thirst as he chopped firewood and took care of some fences that needed work. He broke things to re-fix just to stay out of the house.

As he walked into the house, her scent hit him like he ran full speed into a brick wall. It overpowered him. It had never been that strong before; even his wolf stood on all fours and pushed toward the surface. Jake instinctively followed her scent through the house. He opened his bedroom door and saw the most beautiful creature he'd ever laid eyes on.

Cathryn was naked, laid back on her elbows. He skin glistened like milk chocolate satin. Entranced by the vision in his bed, his breathing labored, perspiration formed on his brow. Her smile took his breath away. She beckoned him with her index finger and those beautiful deep amber eyes.

Jake stood there, unable to move. He and his wolf fought for control, and the man was losing. Jake could do nothing but stare at her as his jeans tightened. He took long deep breaths. Jake shook his head, needing to clear the siren fog she placed in his mind. Finally, he regained his composure.

"Baby, we can't. Not just yet; let's just wait a couple more days. I think we can make love then. Please?"

Cathryn lowered her eyebrows. Her eyes became tiny slits. A loud growl escaped from her throat, her lips pulled back to show her teeth as her canines extended. To say this woman was one pissed off she-wolf was an understatement. Jake stepped back a step when Cathryn stood on his bed to her full height, her arms spread out.

"I'm fine! I told you two day ago! Two weeks ago! The day we came home from the hospital! I'm okay! Especially after I shifted! I'm all healed!"

Cathryn put her hand in the air, palm toward him.

"You know what? Never mind, I'm going to find myself a Navy SEAL! I'm sure one of them will take care of me since every fucking Marine I end up with seems determined to fail to please me!"

Cathryn started to take a step off the bed, but Jake was there within two strides. He grabbed her by the back of her knees and pulled her legs out from under her. Cathryn squealed and was wet before her back hit the mattress, with him right on top of her. Jake pinned her arms above her head then spread her legs wide with his knees.

He stared directly into her eyes. His emerald green eyes glowed brightly. Her eyes were wide with astonishment.

"Look, woman. I love you, but there are some things you don't knock. You can say whatever you want about me, my family, and even my business."

Cathryn gasped when Jake pushed her legs wider and rolled his hips tighter against her sex.

"But you will not disrespect the Corps. You…Get…Me?"

He smiled then settled his hips in between her legs.

"Yes, de…" was all she could get out before he devoured her lips with his in a ravenous kiss.

***

Cathryn's senses overloaded. Jake quickly sat up, removed his clothes, then just as quickly settled himself back in between her legs, covering her body with his. His cock was positioned perfectly at her entrance, without a condom.

Slowly, very slowly, Jake pushed. Cathryn smiled up at him as he seated himself to the hilt. She tried to calm her breathing, but her senses overwhelmed her. The normal tingling sensation increased tenfold. The electricity from their ultimate connection flicked at her nerve endings. Vibrations strummed through her from her head to her toes then settled in her pussy. The wave sent a flood of cream that damn near drowned Jake's cock.

Cathryn felt all of him. His need to claim her, mark her as his mate. She felt his love. His love for her was the reason for his continued existence. His lust, his hunger to make love to her every chance he could. His fears, which terrified him if he had to live without her. His commitment; she felt his all-consuming commitment the most. Through his eyes she saw and felt all of him.

She understood his emotions, his real emotions, as all of her fears washed away. He would never control her. Never stop her from her dreams. She felt his promise to her and their future family. He would always love them. Protect them with his dying breath.

Cathryn nodded "Yes" to his proposal.

Jake smiled. His canines emerged through his gums. Slowly he pulled out, then slammed into her pussy, at the same time he sank his fangs into her shoulder. Cathryn screamed her pleasure as an instant, powerful orgasm caused her pussy to pulsate. Another surge of cream flooded her channel and his cock.

Jake rolled, rocked his hips hard against her. He held tight to her shoulder with his fangs as he grunted and groaned his pleasure.

Cathryn arched her back and screamed his name with each thrust he gave her from the most prolonged, hardest orgasm she had ever experienced in her life.

Jake retracted his fangs, finally released her shoulder, and released his orgasm at the same time he flooded her womb with his seed.

Cathryn's breathing subsided, her heartrate lowered. Jake slowed his rhythm. She basked in the sensations of each of his emotions, and she knew he'd done the same as he felt hers.

He devoured her lips with passion. Reluctantly Jake broke the kiss, gazed into Cathryn's eyes, but kept his rhythm. She caressed his back and grabbed his ass to pull him in deeper.

She felt this was what Jake had waited for. She was the woman of his dreams, and this was what his life was supposed to be. As she knew deep down this was the life she'd always wanted.

"Cathryn, baby, I love you."

"Oh, Jake, sweetheart, I love you, too!" She was no longer afraid of her new perfect life. With the man of her dreams.

If you enjoyed this story, please leave a review where you purchased this book.

I would love to hear from my readers.

cjjonesauthor62@gmail.com

Keep In Touch With CJ:

www.cjjonesauthor.com

www.facebook.com/empathicshifters

www.twitter.com/EmpathicShifter

Made in the USA
San Bernardino, CA
18 April 2018